Four Dervishes

To the memory of Nazir Khan Rind, who bought me
my first book and for Charlotte, who continues to buy me more

Four Dervishes

(چہار درویش)

Hammad Rind

SEREN

Seren is the book imprint of
Poetry Wales Press Ltd,
4 Derwen Road, Bridgend, Wales, CF31 1LH

www.serenbooks.com
facebook.com/SerenBooks
Twitter: @SerenBooks

ISBN: 9781781726310
Ebook: 9781781726327

A CIP record for this title is available from the British Library.

The publisher acknowledges the financial assistance
of the Books Council of Wales.

Printed by Pulsioprint.

Contents

...when he drew near, he saw four erratic *fakirs* with *kafnis* on their bodies, and their head reclined on their knees; sitting in profound silence, and senselessly abstracted. The state was such as that of a traveller, who, separated from his country and his sect, friendless and alone, and overwhelmed with grief, is desponding and at a loss. In the same manner sat these four *fakirs*, like statues, and a lamp placed on a stone burnt brightly; the wind touched it not, as if the sky itself had been its shade, so that it burnt without danger.

Bagh o Bahar, or *The Garden and the Spring*, translated from the Urdu of Mir Amman of Dehli by Duncan Forbes

Fakir or faqir, literally 'poor' in Arabic, Persian and Turkish (fakir) and 'beggar' in Urdu, is sometimes used to signify someone who has renounced worldly possessions.

نمی دانم چه محفل بود ، شب جایی که من بودم

Amir Khusro Dehlavi

A Hairy Beginning

A ND THEN THERE WAS NO LIGHT. The entire world sank into a dark and heavy silence, which lasted for an extremely long moment before being perforated by the hoarse grunts of hundreds of power generators starting up at once. This mechanical lamentation jolted me out of the shock of the abrupt and involuntary plunge into the tenebrous depths of the unknown. I gaped at the black and dead screen of the TV box incredulously and then at the ceiling fan above to find it gradually breaking its rotational cycle. Its erstwhile innumerable wings could now be counted. Two drops of sweat emerged from the back of my head racing each other downward following the vertebrae and the inexplicable rules of gravity. All these signs pointed towards one thing – the electrical heart that pumped power into the various veins and wires of the house had stopped throbbing.

After a few stationary minutes of pointlessly waiting for the power to return, I rose reluctantly to check the fuse-box, but everything seemed to be in order, or so I thought with my little knowledge of electrical matters. I glanced outside to find the streetlamps silent and extinguished in the mourning dusk with their heads hanging low guiltily like convicts in the dock. Although I had a funny feeling all this time and although I didn't want to acknowledge it, it became blatantly evident that the capricious electricity had vanished once again without any warning or notice. Another power-outage, another black-out, another episode of load-shedding. Just because the State, or its incompetent energy department, could not manage its electric supply, every once in a while, they would deprive us from power. But how could it have happened at this time, when the Tache Show was on air – in other words, during the one hour when every citizen would be fixing their ogling sockets at the image-emitting screen to watch their favourite telly show? How could they have done this to me, to us, to the entire nation?

Who doesn't like a soppy, cheesy, soap opera – something larger than this monotonous, humdrum, mean and miserable life of ours – something that would reaffirm your belief in human creativity? I, for one, am hugely fond of the curiously named tele-invention that has no connection to Rossini or Netrebko, for it provides me with plenty on human nature to reflect upon. Oh, and I am Khusro, and I will be your host and storyteller tonight (or today, if you happen to be reading these words on the wrong side of the globe).

The Tache Show was the daily tele-tale broadcasted every evening between 6 and 7 pm about a family of toffs in immaculate suits and sparkling jewellery. Genghis, the chief of this clan, owned millions of acres of fertile agricultural land, stables of faultless steeds, noisy and funny-faced race-cars in hideously glitzy colours and a very bushy moustache, which also served him as the sieve for his soup diet and would have offered an ideal refuge to many birds and rodents, had it been just a shade bushier. A spectacular affair, it was always proudly erect and never droopy (although not so exaggerated, I hasten to add, as the one attributed to Alp Arslan, the Seljuk Sultan, who is believed to have had to tie his moustache behind his head while on the chase or in bed so that it would not get in his way while hunting down a stag or coupling with an odalisque). The fruit of many arduous exercises and special diet programmes, it was kept gauzed under a bandage overnight and at breakfast, fed with a special tonic made of almond oil and buffalo butter. No wonder that the TV programme, originally known as *Sherbet Fort*, after the name of the protagonist's magnificent abode, had come to be casually known as the Tache Show by all and sundry.

And since we're on it, why be miserly with praise – it wasn't just his moustache. His gaze, when he focused it on you, pierced right through from behind the camera, through the tele-screen and to your unsuspecting sofa, would make your legs tremble and jitter like a '60s rock star.

No one could say with utmost certainty as to how long the tele-series had been going on. What I knew for a fact was that I had watched it for all thirty years of my life on this planet. What was more important was how it had become an essential and addictive part of our national life, punctuating the boredom of existence by the perturbations caused every evening by its numerous characters and their many worldly affairs. To see the various escapades and adventures of Genghis on the racecourse, chase or turf, or of his servants cuckolding him in the meanwhile, or in plain words, to witness the exciting drama unfold its manifold mysteries the entire nation would wake up from its deep slumber for an hour. It was a ritual, a tradition, a ceremony of an almost religious status and one of the few which bonded our people together, providing them with icebreakers for chilly, awkward social occasions. During that one hour, life would come to a standstill, nothing happening – all kind of activities, idleness, progress, regression, frolicking, skirt-chasing, fornication, petty crimes, misdemeanours, even felonies – yes, during that one hour burglars would refrain from breaking into the shiny marble bungalows of patricians; murderers would spare the lives of their victims for those sixty minutes. I have heard about many an old-timer who waited for the weekly episode to finish before taking their last breath. And as I said, until that evening, even the callous electrical department had not dared to press that plump, velvety and inviting red button, imagined as the tool of fate which decided if we were to remain in light or darkness. But that evening this final mask of human kindness was lifted from their hideous electrical faces.

Every beginning has the grain of end hidden in its belly and all that ascends has to descend, as they say. The eclipse of Genghis's fortunes – and that of the tele-series with it – had in fact started on the very first episode when Genghis, then a spoilt little brat of fourteen years, had found a grey hair in his waxed, glossy and precocious moustache to the horror of his entire family. But the signs of decay had become particularly more obvious recently when this same moustache – grown to tremendous proportions by now – was massacred while Genghis was attempting to save his favourite hound Roxanna from a fire caused by the disloyal hound-keeper at the instigation of a jealous neighbour. A few harrowing moments later, when Genghis re-emerged on the screen holding the studded collar without Roxanna, the red, incinerated remains on his upper lip looked like a charred battlefield. Now it was a well-known fact that the good old G. owed his pomp and glory to his facial hair and so the audience was made to realise then that the immaculately appearing marble palace had started cracking and would collapse any evening now.

The fairy tales of my childhood were populated by mighty, evil giants, who went around incarcerating inexplicably frail beauties in lofty towers. For all knights-errant in their shining armours the secret to rescuing the damsel was not the straightforward, albeit potentially cumbersome, execution of the evil giant but to slay some unwary parrot, encaged in an impenetrable castle on a far-away island. The symbolic parrot was meant to hold the key to this giant's life in a voodoo-like fashion and by killing the parrot the giant, wherever he might happen to be at that point, would be slain with that same stroke. So, in a similar, though not exactly the same fashion – as his moustache was not located on a far-away island – this thick layer of fur was tacitly known to be the key to our Genghis's life.

As I was saying, on that unusual night something unprecedented happened. The miserable little clerks of the energy department snatched the light from our lives exactly when a bespectacled medicine man was explaining with the help of an x-ray how our bewhiskered hero, who had been lately suffering with hypochondria –an indication of a change in the script-writing staff – could have been afflicted with some mortal condition. The physician's jargon was getting more and more technical, his gestures more and more theatrical, and I had to muster up all of my mental faculties in order to make some sense out of it. But before I could understand whether Genghis had been diagnosed with a tumorous growth in his brain, or whether he was being forced to undergo an important surgery which might leave him tache-less, the world sank into a silently resonant darkness.

The absence of power, which had been troubling us for many years now, had started one day when the rivers of the land had suddenly run dry. The erstwhile sources of life and electricity to millions had taken this measure, perhaps in protest to the various acts of maltreatment by the desperate people who had been pissing and drowning in them. Since that day, the electricity would disappear for hours in a row and would only return like a dishevelled and hungover hag stumbling homewards after a rough night. All this while, the ordinary tasks dependent on electricity would have to halt.

I don't recall how things were before the light disappeared from our lives but by now, the lack of power had become such a normal phenomenon that no one actually complained about this inconvenience. Of course, one would still break into a customary oath every now and then to declare annoyance, or mutter profanities to reveal unsavoury secrets about the private lives of the clerks of the power department. But I had never seen an organised protest against this or any other matter of real significance. In their defence though, the stoic people of this region don't really like to complain anyway.

Now some people blame telly for this widespread complacent attitude. After all, those thousand and one channels are there to provide you with all kinds of entertainment at the slightest touch of your whimsical thumb, bringing this manna to your lazy divan for the entire year without a break. A telly year is a cycle of music contests with tone deaf yodellers brown-nosing the judges to win their short-lived fame, reality programmes with peevish dullards thrown together in dungeons eating each other's minds with their petty squabbles, various ovine creatures bleating and swearing their unimaginative oaths at each other after discovering that the real fathers of their children were also responsible for half of the town's population of imps and stray dogs. This mindless fodder doesn't leave one much time to ponder and certainly no time to complain and if there were no shows like *Sherbet Fort*, where would the poor folks find their entertainment? You can't just blame Far-See or television for everything. After all, it is but a mere screen of glass.

While I reflected on light, shades and facial hair, the multi-purpose room (which had lately been serving as my TV lounge, bedroom and kitchen) kept getting darker, paying no considera-tion to my thoughts. I peered outside the window. The summer sun was still hurling its last rays at the windscreens of the patient automobiles reposing before setting off on some long journey. Inside the house, however, it was becoming hard to differentiate between the sundry objects lying on the floor. I limped through the heavy darkness, bumping into various items of furniture placed without any arrangement, towards the backyard where I had been keeping the power generator. Having reached there, however, I saw the corpse of the generator lying dolefully with its various limbs scattered around. I remembered, to my annoy-ance, how I had ventured to repair and assemble these parts for the past few weeks, each time giving up the futile task in the end.

My general inadequacy in domestic affairs had been the cause of my recent separation with Zuleika, a once promising miniaturist of the Chughtai school, who had turned into a fiendishly practical woman adroit in plumbing, refrigeration and many similar skills, thanks to all the impractical men in her life, including me. She had been expressing her exasperation with me lying in my divan trying to get hold of the fickle muses of inspiration while she did all the chores, a speech bubble with an eye role permanently haloing her wise head. On such occasions, I would retort emphasising on the fact that it was necessary for the nourishment of my artistic and creative personality to move as little as possible in the physical sense – equipping myself with some metaphor to elaborate the point such as a goblet brimming with nectar would spill if moved abruptly or unnecessarily.

'Look Zulu. You don't want my genius to go dry, do you?' I would say to her sometimes.

'Genius my shoe!' she'd retort, 'one of these days I'm outta here. You can stroke your genius yourself then.'

However, I took all her threats of leaving me as playful persiflage, and was quite shocked when one day she hired a man with a van to remove her effects from my house. That day, I had first felt the presence of the little black dot of regret in my heart that had been since increasing every night in size and dimensions.

And while we are on the topic of inspiration, let me say in a few words that at that point of time I was in a desperate need to tame this fickle tease in order to write something scholarly on the occurrence of the 'Idol or Beauty of Machin' in Persian poetry. Specialists of the subject maintain that Machin or 'Not-China' is a legendary land believed to have existed somewhere beyond the musky meadows of *Khatay* or Cathay famous for its ravishing beauties in embroidered fur robes and caravans of silk-laden Bactrian camels. Once going through a dusty and unvisited corner of the state library, I had found some manuscripts, reading which I concluded that this land was in fact equivalent to the modern Manchuria and that the enchanting idols of the classical poetry were forbears of Lily, a Manchurian flute-blower and former fellow-student whom I had fancied during my university days.

This was at best a personal discovery of minor significance but having somehow convinced myself of its universal utility, I had spent the last six or so months reading between the lines of Farrukhi, Khaqani and other classical Persian poets in a vain attempt to produce a scholarly work, which I was certain, would prove my argument. During all this time, all I had managed to write was the first three pages thanking Zuleika, who had to listen to my theories. My inability to bring forth anything mainly owed to a greater dilemma I was facing, namely the choice of an appropriate style to write this work. I spent most of my time deciding whether I could write my thesis without using the letter e, like an Oulipian, or in a pointless way – that is, without a dot or point like the work of Faizi, a poet at Akbar's court. Needless to say, this work was not going anywhere. Nonetheless, it gave me a great pretext to stay on my divan memorising medieval poetry and looking at my notes all day long while various shows on the goggle-box puked out unwanted entertainment and Zuleika would oil the creaking hinges and mend the broken machinery around the house.

Her departure was still a fresh wound and I had spent every day since the separation trying to forget the various aspects of her personality in vain – facts that had been hitherto hidden from me, though having been right before my eyes, such as her own artistic career that she had to put off due to my lethargy. Besides, my helpless bachelorhood only accentuated her memory by many degrees. Some evenings would drag and just refuse to transpire into mornings. An even more unbearable thought was that if she was still there with me, we could be watching the Tache Show together, thanks to her mending and repairing expertise.

The whole house was sunk in a dark silence punctuated by the intermittent war cries of mosquitoes. It was the month of Temmuz, when this horny hussy is mostly active injecting her malarial serum into the living through her pointy proboscis. After Nisan, this little fly takes a career break for two months owing to her own temporary death by the scorching summer wind, known as *loo* in Urdu. But as soon as the first drop of Savan showers touches the thirsty womb of the sizzling sand, she rises from the dead like a vampire in old Balkan legends. Once someone asked a mosquito why she is not seen in the winter and the little wit retorted in her classic devilish style: "Nobody accords me any respect in the summer. Do you think they'd worship me in the winter?" But despite the universal derision accorded to the little fly, I'd have to concede with the erudite Urdu writer, Khwaja Hasan Nizami, who gives the little intrepid soldier the due credit of valour for announcing her arrival by humming her slightly off-key arias before launching her attack.

I cannot be sure as to whether it was the lack of light and the ensuing darkness or the painful memories of Zuleika or even not being able to continue tonight's episode of the Tache Show, but something was making me exceedingly depressed. As a poet from another and more sentimental century would have said, melancholy tiptoed in stealthily and laid a heavy stone at my heart. I felt a huge gap in my life opening its mouth wider with each passing moment. I knew that I must find a way to stop this gaping mouth from rupturing its jaws. Not knowing how to stop the depressing feeling, I decided to seek guidance from one of my favourite oracles. I picked up the divan of Mirza Ghalib for divinational guidance and to find my answer in the words of the sage. Opening on a random page – well, not entirely random, I had saved, it seemed, a fading discount coupon for a meal in a local fast-food eatery, which had expired last winter, adding to my annoyance – and placing my finger on a random line, I read:

دل پھر طواف کوئے ملامت کو جائے ہے

Dil phir tavāf-e kū-ye malāmat ko jāye hai: 'The heart once again wants to be the pilgrim of the alley of notoriety.'

I could agree no more with the divine Mirza. I had to entertain my heart. The possibility thrilled me and chased the
melancholic thoughts away. I grabbed the weekly entertainment
mag *Sepid-o-Siyah* to find out what was happening in the theatre-
land. I ruled out the snake charmer and the flatulist shows. Then
I remembered the exotic singer, reported to have recently arrived
in the Two Dusky Mares cabaret from Kashmir or Texas or some
other foreign place and who, due to her charming voice and
coquettish manners, had already become the talk of the town.
Perhaps spending a couple of hours listening to this fabled bulbul
would enliven my glum spirit! Thinking this and not trusting the
unpredictable Savan weather, I put a caliph's hood on and slipped
out in the gloomy dusk.

Three Falling Mughals

LAST NIGHT'S SHOWERS had turned the slants and slopes of the street into murky puddles. I hopped over a running stream of rainy scum disturbing a horde of tiny insect warriors. A conspiracy of rooks was heading noisily westward to witness the red globe of the sun sink in its own blood. The garish chariot of the solar deity, in the hasty flight to its nightly lodging, had dropped some of its molten gold in the black ooze, which was finding its way to the wide-open lidless gutters. Notes of some old ballad escaped out of a loft skylight riding on the wind's shoulders.

I decided to take a shortcut through the old neighbourhood of rope-makers. The day's work had long finished and the little workshops were all closed for the night but the air in the narrow streets of the quarter was powdery with tiny grains of jute, making it hard to breathe and punctuating my reveries with the erratic fits of coughing. This land produces excellent jute, which is used to make supple and svelte ropes for hanging all kinds of objects and creatures but mainly to be employed by the local funambulists, tricksters, *jamooras*, suiciders and executioners. The industrious artisans of this wonderful city spend hours twisting ropes, which could possibly end in a noose around their own necks. Capital punishment is still very much in vogue and the weekly public hangings are one of the most visited tourist attractions of the country – our country, Saqia, a land which knows how to keep its traditions alive.

For the last six or seven centuries, we have been striving to survive in our beloved πατρίδα. Life is hard like a rock, fragile like an eggshell, hot like a frying pan, dusty like a racecourse and stagnant like a pond buzzing with mosquitoes. People here just want to live peacefully and do not usually interfere in each other's affairs unless poked by someone else first, which is a common occurrence.

Since time immemorial, the dynasty of Saqids has been ruling this little enclave of land pressed between its more self-satisfied neighbours. The legend of the family's ascension to power is one of fascination, intrigue, mystery, romance and action.

Once upon a time, there was a king, who was more interested in stars – celestial, not their more ephemeral human imitation – than warfare; stars, which would one day, be the cause of his final fall and at that point his, Humayun's, father would not be there to sacrifice his own life to save his firstborn. In fact, Humayun was not the first in his illustrious family to die of a fall. His grandfather, Umar Sheikh Mirza, king of the Fergana valley and beyond, had also met his fate, having fallen from the lofty pigeon-house on his castle into the encircling moat. 'His soul flew away like a pigeon,' Umar's son and the first Timurid-Mughal emperor of India, Babur, would later describe the tragic incident in his autobiography.

In another life, Humayun, a prince then, had fallen ill, struck with such a severe malady that in spite of all their medicinal potions and *majūns*, all skilled physicians of the realm had to apologise to his father, Babur, and admit their defeat at the hands of a cruel fate. Legend-whisperers say that at that point, the first Great Mughal decided to sacrifice his own life to save his son's. The story goes that Babur circled around his son's deathbed seven times to take his illness upon himself repeating the formula *bardâshtam* ('I took it over'), following an ancient belief of his people. Lo and behold, on the seventh round, Babur, the imperial father, collapsed and Humayun, the auspiciously-named heir apparent, opened his eyes.

This wouldn't be the only time that the life of Humayun, the starstruck emperor, would be saved by another man. After his forces had been routed by the rebel and self-acclaimed Sher Shah Suri, the Lion King, in the battle of Chausa, the defeated emperor had to jump into the River Ganges to flee from the battlefield, only realising too late that he did not know how to swim. If it was not for Nizam the *Saqqa* ('Water-Carrier'), who happened to be filling his water-skin from the murky river at this significant point in Indian and Saqian history, the name of the House of Tamburlane in India would have drowned in the *Ganga* only fifteen years after its inception. Having laid the unconscious Mughal on his leather skin, Nizam successfully swam across the river and took him to his humble hut, where he and his family revived His Highness by rubbing his royal palms and soles. Nizam was rewarded in return by being allowed to rule over the Timurid Empire for one day. Humayun soon realised, however, that it was a rather unwise decision when the *Saqqa* managed to bankrupt the treasury by issuing leather coins – so great was his love for the material used to manufacture his water-skins. But it was too late now. Sher Shah was at the city gates and the throne of India was once again about to change hands.

Humayun spent the next fifteen years in Persia as a guest of Safavid Shah, Tahmasp, trying to woo him with the most delicious lentil dishes his Indian chefs prepared with the right amount of garlic and cumin fried in *ghee*. Meanwhile, Sher Shah built roads and post offices and named his favourite type of mango Chausa after the battlefield where he had defeated the ill-fated Mughal. But as soon as the mango-loving Sher Shah died, Humayun returned with Persian armies to win his empire back. Nizam the Water-Carrier hastily came to kiss the feet of the right-ful emperor of India. He had never accepted the usurper's rule, he declared. Humayun smiled. Always remembering his benefac-tors and forgetting their follies, Humayun rewarded the *Saqqa* once again, granting him a large estate, one thousand and one *parganas* to be exact. This estate, snugly placed between Persia and India, was to become the kingdom of Saqia, which is still ruled by the progeny of the first water-carrying king, in the memory of whose vocation, the state emblem is a water-skin. *Saqqa*'s son, however, and to the father's great dismay, turned out to be an erudite scholar. As a lover of literary themes, he changed his father's *Saqqa* into more poetic *Saqi* or Cupbearer and since his time, all kings of his line have been called Saqi and the kingdom Saqia. This cup-bearing king was also a great administrator, who built a wall around the small country to save it from any possible future invasions. The Great Wall of Saqia now serves as a brick and stone billboard for marketing international imports, as well as a public urinal.

The events taking place in its more important neighbouring states have also left their due impact on the little kingdom. Fully aware of their humble and diminutive status in contrast to that of their mightier neighbours, the Saqid dynasty managed to remain loyal to both the Timurid and the Safavid courts and could in this way save their little state from being swallowed by either side. This policy was continued after the advent of the European colonisers – or *Farangi* ('Franks') as they were initially called and later rechristened as *Angrez* ('English'). Thus, whilst one of the Saqi princes assisted the Blighty Sahibs crush the Mutiny of Sepoys, caused by the local disgust for pork and beef, his brother accompanied the dethroned Mughal emperor Bahadur Shah Zafar or Brave King Victory in his exile to Rangoon, following Victory's defeat by the British.

Saqia was recognised as a princely state in the Raj period. Members of its ruling family were appointed to assume unimportant rubber-stamp roles in both India and Persia and were duly entitled Falan Bahadur or Folânoddowleh by the neighbouring empires. Thanks to its capable statesmen, it managed to maintain its sovereignty during and after the partition of India, when all the other princely states were being swallowed by the scions of the erstwhile India.

This fertile land has not forgotten the knack of producing able statesmen. The current premier, for example, is truly the master of all trades. His CV or course of life boasts of such diverse vocations and skills as having twice served as the Chief Mountebank, a milkman, a bear-baiter, a professional leper and a real-estate agent amongst many others. Besides such a variety of professional careers, he has been, from time to time and betwixt serious jobs, an amateur thespian. In his fortieth year, he had a near-death experience when he fell from the fourth-storey bedroom window of a council flat, inhabited by, amongst others, a woman of famed mystique, on the sudden and unexpected arrival of her husband. Having landed on his four feet with a feline ability he didn't hitherto know he possessed, he decided there and then that if the Almighty had saved his life that day it was meant to be devoted to a greater cause and thus he entered into the public sphere and within a short while was elected the premier. A genuinely self-made man, he climbed his way from a petty scoundrel to the first person of the country. He now owns many offshore companies registered in Delaware and the Bermuda triangle, and is a source of inspiration for the youth and the OAPs alike.

Our Lady of the Golden Nose

I HAD REACHED THE THEATRE-LAND of the city now. There was a discouragingly long and unsurprisingly misshapen queue outside Two Dusky Mares. Perhaps due to the power cut or maybe owing to the fame of the Kashmiri or Texan warbler, every man and woman seemed to have found their way to the cabaret. I tried to find a vulnerable point to cut the queue but failing that and not being in the mood to spend the next few hours waiting in the belly of a slowly crawling human serpent, I decided to wander about in the neighbourhood to kill time when a throng of narcissistic photographers with tenacious beggars hanging on their sleeves attacked me.

I hope you can empathise with the strong misanthropic feelings which had enveloped me completely by this point. Then, as if in a moment of epiphany, I realised how close I was to the central cemetery. I don't know why but the thought cheered me up tremendously. Perhaps I just wanted to escape the living and take refuge amongst the dead. My nose started itching with excitement as I started walking towards the Neo-Mudejar arches and belfries of the shrine of Our Lady of the Sacred Nose –*Pak-Nak Khatun* in Urdu – situated at the entrance of the cemetery.

This once majestic building is still a landmark that can be spotted from far away. It was constructed by one of the illustrious ancestors of the current king, Saqi VII, during the last century in the memory of a foreign saint, Shahnaz of Shahpur, who had chosen our humble land to spend the last years of her life.

Connected to two most eminent families of a neighbouring land through birth and marriage, she had led the most serene and uneventful life before her husband started suspecting her of being romantically involved with another. He challenged her before the elders of both families, who decided to judge the matter through trials of fire and water. She was given many opportunities to prove her innocence. Sadly, she failed all. She was made to walk on coals. She is said to have cried and writhed with pain, which was enough to prove her guilt. She was asked to speak in her defence. She stubbornly refused to utter a word. The poor judges were left helpless. The toothless elders pronounced their verdict through frightfully shaking beards. The ancient and most just Code of Hammurabi was applied to Shahnaz's nose, the sign of honour in many societies, which was amputated by her own husband.

She neither uttered a sound of protest nor blinked with pain when the nose was removed from her face, leaving two inhuman gashes in its spot. I'd advise you to take what I'm going to say next with a grain of salt, but legend-whisperers claim that since that moment Shahnaz the Rhinometa never once blinked in her life nor did she ever sleep a wink. A faithful servant quietly brought her to Saqia, where having rented out a little room at the site destined to be her final resting place, the two women decided to spend the rest of their days quietly. Only it was not meant to be so.

Soon the fame of a noseless lady, who never shut her lids, spread far and wide and the devoted people of Saqia, who have always been reverent to foreign saints, especially those who can perform miracles, started coming to her door in throngs to seek blessings and make offerings. She would receive everyone with the same blank expression in her eyes and without uttering a word would cure the chronic and obstinate maladies with a miraculous touch. Her most astounding miracle was her contributions to the physical aesthetics of her visitors and many upper-crust *Khanums* from Shemran would visit her to have their unwieldy trunks turned into a Roman aquiline or a cute impish upturned nose according to the latest fashion. A handful of jealous plastic surgeons, who had the audacity to submit a formal complaint against her in the civil court, met with people's ire and women's heels. The King ordered the best goldsmith in the land to fix a golden nose for the Rhinometa but the night before the operation was due, Shah-nose, who had not closed her eyes for more than four years, finally shut them tight never to open them again. The team of surgeons who performed the post-mortem reported that she had overtired herself. She was barely thirty years old. The golden nose was fixed to the corpse's lifeless face, lending its name to the shrine.

Her story, however, does not end with her death. Pilgrims kept coming to ask for blessings from the dead saint and making their offerings on her grave and to facilitate their pilgrimage, the King left no expense on the construction of this shrine. A Castellan company of architects was selected to design the building after a very tough competition, resulting in the popularity of Neo-Mudejar style throughout the kingdom for religious and secular buildings. In the meanwhile, the former husband of the Noseless Lady of the Golden Nose, regretting his terrible act with much ostentation, moved to the kingdom crying and lamenting how unfortunate he had been to lose his wife and she to lose her nose, which was all a combined conspiracy of their mutual enemies, stars and fate. Thus, somehow proving himself innocent of the rhinomatic offence, he became the guardian of the shrine. The poor widower had a weakness for wedding ceremonies and thus he got married several times and sired innumerable children, whose descendants are still a respectable clan in our country. They are, however, seldom seen around the shrine, to which they owe much of their prestige.

These days the old building is mainly frequented by owls, bats and fornicators. Some of the parts have fallen into ruins due to floods, earthquakes and lack of care by the responsible authorities. The right wing completely collapsed owing to an earthquake five years ago and the majority of people believed that it was due to the sinful excesses being committed by the adulterers of the realm who held their trysts in the shady corners of the Sacred Nose. Now most people maintain that the abundance of sins and ensuing earthquakes are yet another sign of the imminent arrival of the Doomsday. However, until all the other signs foretold in traditions and legends are seen one by one, we could safely enjoy our last days on this planet.

'The Lady must have been quite a ravisher in her day,' an irreverent reverie trespassed my mind whilst glancing at the portraits and icons on the walls of the shrine – an oval face harmonised with sharp chiselled features, guarding olive eyes with a feline peculiarity chasing the onlooker and best of all, a cleft chin like the final stroke on a masterpiece, the signature of a satisfied creator – like the ones which adorned the delightful faces of Ava Gardner, Stefania Sandrelli, the Queen of Sheba, Nahid Akhtar, the King of Sheba, Virginia O'Brien and one of the Redgraves – a feature much lauded and invoked by classical Persian poets.

My thoughts were still stuck in that divine little fosse, when my eyes stopped at an unexpected face – it was a 'Wanted' poster incongruously stuck amongst the otherwise perfectly feminine gallery and describing a short career résumé of the most famous local outlaw, Haji Hoja Mirza Zoltan Khan Pasha or Zoltan in short. A street urchin had covered the chin of the wanted man with a long bushy beard, which had somehow engulfed the criminal's face with an aura of piety. 'Zoltan,' I thought, 'Now that must be a fascinating character with many stories to tell!'

Despite being a bandit and an outlaw, the man was known more as a hero, someone transported from the age of chivalry, like a romantic Robin Hood and a courageous Coeur de Lion, who allegedly robbed the wealthy to dispense the spoils amongst the poor. There were several stories around of his adventures and charitable acts, the most famous of which went something along the lines of his saving the honour of a respectable family by fighting a bear with his bare hands. According to the most reliable reports of this famous incident, once during his adventures, he had stumbled upon a grizzly bear – some said it was an unshapely immigrant – molesting the supposedly virgin daughter of an old impoverished king, who had somehow changed his career to become a beggar. Zoltan had thrashed the immigrant and helped the king get his throne back. According to some other equally reliable reports, it was the daughter of the ugly immigrant who was being molested by the beggar-king and Zoltan had helped the immigrant with his immigration paperwork, at the same time thrashing the beggar.

There were numerous accounts of how he had brought many corrupt politicos to book. His name became the byword for the concept of vigilante justice. People lynched criminals in his name. Amongst teenagers, the cause of his fame, however, lay on his on-and-off scandals with the steatopygian Armenian socialite Marina *Quat'-Culs*, the eldest of the notorious Bratian sisters, and on the many stories of his nocturnal triumphs, which had made him into the very epitome of virility. Rumour had it that he had once satisfied a dozen sturdy country wenches in one night without once waning. But to the simple people of these lands, the most endearing aspect of this virile outlaw was the tragic aura around his fame. Had he not lost his own sister in a tragic and unnatural accident? Nevertheless, all these charitable deeds or personal tragedies didn't seem to impress the law-enforcing authorities of the state, which had set a huge reward on Zoltan's head.

'100,000 d. to anyone who brings this man to the dock dead or alive!' the announcement read in bold letters. I tried to decode the curriculum vitae of the legend in the failing light, but the lines had been made illegible by the editorial work of an amateur hand, probably of the same street Arab, who seemed to have a proclivity of using the text-jargon. '#Zoltan was here,' I managed to decipher a badly written line.

Verdi and Djinns

A S SOON AS I STEPPED into the cemetery, I felt at peace with myself as if a huge burden had been lifted off my shoulders and I had left every care and worry outside these four walls. I felt envious of the inhabitants of the necropolis for being exempted from having cumbersome interactions with the living, to have vacuous conversations and to fulfil the arbitrary responsibilities imposed by the society.

Tombstones were fixed in the ground at an almost equal distance facing in the same direction as if expecting someone or waiting for the trumpet to blow on the Doomsday, which would allow the dead to leave their graves. I have always found the inscriptions on these tombstones highly inspiring. I can imagine, nay almost see, the excited look on the face of my reader imagining me as one of those sick aficionados of the necropolis. Forgive me if I disappoint you but I merely love peace and solitude, which is sadly only available in cemeteries these days.

Brevity or fragility of life is the most common theme of the religious dictums or the poetic verses carved on these epitaphs. For some life is but a span, for some a dream, a bubble, or a cookie. بستی اپنی حباب کی سی ہے *Hasti apni habāb ki si hai*: 'A bubble is our life'; ما همه فانی و بقا بس تراست *Mâ hama fâni o baqâ bas Tu-râst*: 'We are all mortal, only You will remain'; جهان افسانه در آلدانما باقی *cihân afsanedir aldanma Bâki*: 'The world is a fable. O Bâki, do not be deceived'; انگار که هر چه نیست در عالم هست *Ingâr ke har-che hast dar âlam nêst*: 'As if whatever in this world exists, doesn't exist'. I realised that it was getting a drop too depressing. I looked round for something more cheerful. Unrequited love and post-mortal affairs also seemed quite popular – سر قبر جوانان لاله رویه دمی که گلرخان آیند به گلگشت *sar-e qabr-e javânân lâla roya dame ke gulrukhân âyand ba gulgasht*: 'Tulips grow at the graves of the young when the rose-cheeked visit for a stroll'; *Die Toten stehn auf, der Tag des Gerichts.*

Some tombstones had the genealogical trees – with branches going all over the place – of some noble bones buried under them. One had a daffodil and the Celtic cross of a Welsh wanderer. Some had tulips and turbans signifying them as the shrines of some minor saints. One would assume that these bones, having exhausted their energies during their living days above ground of stretching to reach stars would stop growing after death. However, the presence of some prehistoric and several yards long graves was clearly defying this line of reasoning. Some say martyrs of religious crusades were buried under these monstrous protractions. Others claim that people used to have gigantic measurements in the past.

I was wandering like an aimless soul thinking about the possibility of post-mortal romances when I heard some voices in the distance. My first reaction, frankly, was one of annoyance about being chased by the living into the city of the silent. After all, I had taken refuge there just to flee from the pestering throngs of humanity and they were there too. Then I remembered that the local rags had been resonant with the news of spirits seen – or rather sensed in the words of the (third) eye-witnesses – around the cemetery in the past few months. Last week they were showing a reality telly-show about vampires infecting their victims with AIDS and other kinds of virusful vermin. I know the sceptic reader of the age of refrigerator and automobile would have trouble believing in the presence of the 'others': spirits, kind or evil, revenants from the past or visitors from the future, aliens from unidentified flying saucers or yeti monks from Tibetan heights, blue djinns of the desert or the wish-fulfilling genie of the lamp, Welsh *pwcas* or wailing Banshees of the Celts, ghouls or *devs* with gigantic proportions, *chüreyls* with their feet turned backwards, one-legged Athenian Empusas or three-legged Zoroastrian zebras, imps or *chalavas* that would jump on your shoulders from trees, trees that weep blood, men with horns, tails and hoofs, shape-shifting hobgoblins or protean *baldanders*, loony werewolves or hirsute *garous*, weasels that turn into badgers or cobras that turn into sultry actresses after having lived for hundreds of years, Occitan horses that kidnap urchins, Heike crabs containing the gouty spirits of slain samurai, fallen angels, dead rising from their graves, dancing skeletons and voices in your head. But in this instance, as well as many others, I like to take the middle path of the Saqi people, who like the ancient Romans and the mediaeval Mongols, respect the deities and demons of all nations so as to avoid the wrath of the true ones by unwittingly declaring them as false.

In the Orient, one is brought up on the stories of djinns, fairies and ghouls by one's parents in order to curb that disobedient streak that children are known to show sometimes. The wayward child hell-bent on throwing tantrums in public for not getting his favourite *qulfi* ice-cream is silenced by his mother who threatens to invoke djinns to kidnap him. The fear, however, is not shed with the age. Wise and worldly grown-ups prefer to assume the convenience of explaining the incomprehensible natural phenomena by attributing them to these supernatural powers. At times, though, the supernatural invites itself into our lives.

When I was a child, my grandaunt told me bedtime stories of the adventures of her grandfather, Aliverdi, a renowned *nauha-khan* or performer of dirges. Born in a well-reputed family of royal jesters, he had his career lined up for him. All he needed was to follow his ancestors' mirthful profession and to make his regal audience laugh with the ages-old gags and jokes with punchlines that never failed to do their trick. But inexplicably, he turned out to be nothing like his ancestors and had a strange partiality to wailing, which defied all kinds of logical or illogical reasoning.

It was first discovered one summer, his eighth to be precise, when his uncles and their families were visiting his home before setting off for the famous comedy fringe. One day while the grown-ups were all rehearsing their juggling, stand-up, clown routines, he took his cousins to his room, where he entertained them by singing old ballads about Candy Mountains and unrequited passions that he had lately been listening to on the antediluvian, family-size radio. That afternoon, after having brought the little guests to an utmost tearful state he showed them proudly to the grown-ups, who were at first merely perplexed. Following a series of similar incidents, however, the painful realisation dawned upon his parents that their only son was a pursuant of morose themes: a freak in a family of buffoons. They also realised that he had never ever smiled once in his eight years and had shown no interest in learning the jocular art of his ancestors. They tickled, cajoled and bribed him, and failing that scolded, reprimanded and thrashed him to persuade him to pursue more chucklesome affairs but it was all to no avail. They tried to hide this alien and freakish skill of his from their relations but the little Aliverdi had now started performing in birthday parties, and family gatherings. In his defence, he seemed to have no control over it. Whenever he found himself amongst company, doleful notes would spring out of his throat with the spontaneity of a mountain stream, forcing those present to bawl to their hearts' fill. In a short while, he had become so skilful that he could make people weep their eyes out by the slightest grimace or distortion of his famously expressive face without emitting the slightest noise from his mouth. Soon the inevitable that his parents had feared for so long transpired. At a wedding ceremony, the elders of the family banished Aliverdi from attending any family functions thenceforward, after realising that they had been wailing for two hours listening to his mournful tunes about the death of Mirza the Eloper at the hands of his lover's brothers. Being thus ostracised by his clan and losing the support of his helpless parents he had to think about standing on his own feet and earn his own bread. He decided to do so by busking outside metro stations, making the commuters burst into tears before they jumped into their trains.

A devout man, his repertoire consisted of threnodies, elegies and dirges, *marsiyas, nauhas* and *sozes*, he composed himself about the Battle of Karbala or *Karb-o-Bala* ('Pain and Strife') in dedication to the family of the Third Imam betrayed by the treacherous Kufids and martyred in the desert, and whose daughters were later imprisoned in dark Damascene dungeons. For the first ten days of the Sacred Month, he performed in the greatest centres of the Faithful east of Khurasan – Amroha Sadat, Lucknow, Haiderabad Dakkan, Mahmudabad, Golkanda, Gulbarga, Sehvan, Multan and my own ancestral village of Najafabad Kalra. On the days not marked by the tradition, he sang mournful ballads on other gloomy themes such as the memory of the valiant Hector's carcass being dragged behind Achilles' haughty chariot and the image of the old, blinded Belisarius begging in Byzantium after having been humiliated by his ungrateful master.

Soon his fame reached far and he was invited to perform before His Most Serene Highness, who bestowed upon him the enviable title of the Verdi of Woe, also awarding him with a Fabergé egg, both of which have been passed down in my family. Grandpa Verdi was also known as Graf of Grief in the West and *Emir-i Hüzün* and *Anis-e Sâni* in the East. Despite all the fame and prosperity, he never forgot his busking past, however, and never returned a seeker empty-handed. When once approached by a beggar and not finding on his person any change or bankcards to give him, he took off his embroidered, perfumed shirt and handed it to the astonished mendicant. His ancestors had raised a huge fortune by splitting people's sides – by making people shed bucketfuls of salty tears he made it possible for his progeny to live prosperously for many generations without having to move from their couch.

The first Lord Verdi of Woe had to travel long expanses galloping astride his faithful mare throughout the seven *iqlims* or climates of the globe. During his travels, he befriended many famous people, had affairs with many starlets of the silver screen and fought duels with forces of darkness. My favourite tale of all his adventures was the one about his visit to the Holy See. My grandaunt used to emphasise here how this particular journey had been ominous from the beginning. Aliverdi's wife had just whispered in his ear that she was pregnant with what she believed was a baby or two, and in his state of elation, he had forgotten to take his usual travel accoutrement – *harmal* capsules, onion bulbs, garlic pills, hair of jackal – charms supposed to protect one from the unseen catastrophes.

Aliverdi was passing through a dense, sunless jungle when he lost his way and stumbled upon a village with rather peculiar inhabitants. The villagers, in strange garish and gaudy garments, took him to the chief of the tribe. This hoary enturbaned man congratulated my surprised forefather on his fame, which had obviously reached their little village. Then he eagerly expressed his wish to hear the famous account of the bravery of Abbas the Ghazi, peace be upon him and his progeny – the brother and loyal flag-bearer of the Third Imam, peace be upon him and his progeny, and his 70-man army – who had fought valiantly without arms in order to quench the thirst of his young niece in the scorching heat and the desert plain of Karbala. At this point, my grandaunt would recite and declaim the entire *marsiya*, assuming a solemn tone calling to mind battle drums and hoofs, arching her eyebrows on each guttural letter. The doleful tale of the valiant but caring uncle attempting to fill his *mashkiza* or water-skin from the Euphrates but getting his arms chopped off instead by the enemies brought an Oxus to the chief's eyes and those present could not help but break into a full-blown ceremony of mourning and wailing.

After the wailing affair, Aliverdi was duly treated to a hearty banquet in his honour, with villagers bringing him a massive heap of the most scrumptious *gosfand pulao* and *shami kebabs* he'd ever tasted in his life. The more he ate from the heap and filled his stomach from this manna, the more it grew in quantity. After having savoured this delicious delight for hours, Aliverdi Khan reluctantly decided to leave his meal to resume it in the morning. He went to sleep in the tent of the chief and 'lo and behold' – as my grandaunt would say in her attempt to surprise her attentive listener with the grand finale – when he woke up in the morning, he found himself lying under a solitary date palm in an infinite sandy plain. There were no tents or villagers in sight. In fact, the whole village had disappeared, like Persian from India. There were vultures circling above his head and the plate lying beside him was filled with a heap of dry cow dung, witnessing which it slowly dawned upon our perplexed dirge-singer that he had been a guest of no less than the chief of djinns himself, having enjoyed the reputed hospitality of these fiery creatures. For it is a known fact that djinns can only eat waste and excrement and cannot digest food which has not been previously processed through an animal's guts and expelled through its cavities.

So, I was saying that I was in the cemetery, where I had heard some voices and which I now decided to follow, being overwhelmed by curiosity. On a second thought, after all, it could just be some poor man's funeral ceremony and throwing a handful of dust on someone's coffin is the least one can do to pay one's respects to the departed. Although burials are generally performed during the day, on certain occasions the bereaved would like to bury the deceased at a late hour. Sometimes it is due to practical reasons. In the hot climes of our land flesh starts rotting soon after death and preserving it by using huge blocks of ice doesn't always help and although in the imitation of the West, many morgues have lately opened their business, most people are still a bit sceptical about leaving their dear departed at these cold storages. Besides, there is no ideal time prescribed in the scriptures or law for a burial and if someone wants to bury their dead so late and if the gravedigger, Zeno, doesn't mind then why should you or I?

Ah, hang on a minute. Before we take this turn around this grove of date-palms to see what's happening behind it, let me avail of this opportunity to introduce you to the most popular gravedigger of my city. Zeno is a very thoughtful green-eyed youth, possibly in his twenties or thirties and famed to be exceedingly skilled at what he does. His style of digging is smooth, slinky and graceful, which according to some, is out of consideration for the grief of the bereft and the peace of the departed. He carries on digging, hollowing, emptying the bowels of earth with his spade without the slightest grumble. And incidentally, a rather trivial but interesting point before we move on: he also happens to be of some foreign extraction (as one can guess from his foreign-sounding name) and the fact that an alien like him can enjoy such an extremely desired job is a proof of the principle of equal opportunities being implemented at every level in Saqia.

Right! Now that we know at least one person who we can chance upon in this cemetery without causing much social awkwardness, let's find out the cause of these mysterious voices. So as I had rightly predicted, it was indeed a burial party, and a very small, unassuming one at that: a woman in a Gothic cloak carefully holding a bundle of black silk and a man in a feathered hat were standing quietly around a hole which was fast turning into a grave with each new movement from Zeno's sharp shovel, who was busily widening the mouth of the hungry earth to make it another offering. A rather dismal idea came to my mind about how one hardly realises while strutting about arrogantly on the surface of this earth that one will eventually end up beneath it one day. Revenge of the petty and vindictive earth, eh? But who had died? There was no coffin, no corpse.

Zeno had dug out the grave deep enough to conceal his entire lower half in it. He looked at the woman, who bent down to pass him the silk bundle – a small morsel for the earth to swallow. Back to the womb whence it came. Zeno laid the bundle carefully on the grave floor and leaped out of the grave like a nimble cat. The woman broke into muffled sobs. Zeno started filling the gaping hole up with quick, sharp movements of his spade. No one had paid any attention to me so far. Nonetheless, I approached them to throw a handful of dust on the pyramidal mound. Once the grave had been satisfactorily built, I looked closely at the two strangers. The woman was in a long black leather cloak with an astrakhan collar, popular amongst Goths. However, in the failing light it was difficult to determine whether the cut was Ostrogothic or Visigothic. Despite the gloom in the air, I could not help noticing that her knees were peeping through her black designer trousers. The man was in tattered clothes, which seemed to have seen better days. An almost deplumed hat with a half-eaten feather was on his head.

The twilight sky, which had been looking distraught for a while, suddenly burst into tears, weeping like a wimpy child. In a short while, the rain was accompanied by stony hails reminding me of a superstition from my schooldays about the volley of icy shot hurled down by the angry sky leaving a permanent dent in one's head. The fickle monsoon had gathered its brass and wind to pump out a somewhat pompous funeral march. The stormy wind started lashing our faces. The lightening was flashing in a threatening way. The two strangers looked around to find a shelter. Zeno, the foreign gravedigger, who had been collecting his tools, looked up at us for a second, then beckoned us to follow him.

Although it can't have been more than a few steps from the little tomb, but we were drenched to the skin by the time we entered the rather cosy albeit sombre abode of the gravedigger. There was an extensive network of cobwebs at the entrance, which Zeno blamed on the agility of the native arachnids. The living room was carpeted with a tattered rug. Zeno pushed the light button and seeing it refusing to comply, lit some tallow candles, all the while cursing under his breath over the incompetency of the electricity department.

Meanwhile, as we were all settling down on the rug, I examined the over-bloated room with the huge pile of books towering in a corner which had instantly monopolised my gaze and attention. There were some books on existentialism; quite a few burial manuals such as *Bury your Own Dead for Dummies*, *What will Happen after Death* and *Burial Kit 101*; some classics from antiquity, the Dark and Bright Ages, predominantly Pindar and Pliny, *The Maqamat or Assemblies* by al-Hariri of Basra and *The Book of Songs* by Isfahani, and some later works mainly by Swift, Rabelais, Dehkhoda, *Hamzanama* and *Rindnama*. On further scrutiny, a *charpaï* cot-bed made of closely woven palm leaves made itself visible out of the bookish pile.

On the shelves lay some knick-knacks and paraphernalia related to various necessities of life such as a sewing kit, carpenter's tools, fishing lines, laboratory apparatus, lumps of alum, beakers containing powders and fluids and labelled HNO3, *aqua regia* and so on. One of the doors led to an inner chamber and had two Venetian masks with silly and grotesque faces each representing comedy and tragedy. The walls were decorated with kitschy prints of *putti* and cupids frolicking in mud while motherly figures of presumptive Madonnas and Venuses gloated at them lovingly, at the same time admonishing them with their index fingers.

The sudden shower had brought the temperature down and when Zeno placed an invitingly pleasant blazer on the rug, we all huddled around it. He put a samovar on the red coals. Soon the pleasant aromas of mint and cinnamon drifted slowly around the room.

Leila's Knees

HE WAS A PART OF MY BODY, a piece of my flesh. For nine months, I had kept him close to my soul nurturing him with my own blood,' the Gothic woman grumbled softly as she studied the red burning coals. I looked around to see everyone with their heads down seeming sheepish as if by participating in the burial ceremony of that little child, we had somehow been responsible for its demise too.

'It was His will,' I repeated the clichéd formula.

'And yet, if it wasn't for my wretched knees I wouldn't be here,' she said as if she hadn't heard me, leaving me slightly amazed at the incongruity of her statement. I looked at her expecting some sign of grief that might have made her utter those words, but she looked perfectly calm and serene although a bit faint and worn-out. Something in her appearance struck a spark of recognition in my mind but I failed to remember where I had seen her face. She must have been in her twenties or perhaps thirties, I cannot be certain. As you may have guessed, I'm no judge of age, for I believe people can hide their true age by means of various tricks and devices and, besides, internal seasons can just as much cause wrinkles or creases on someone's face as the passing of winters or autumns. Whilst there was something distinctly foreign about her, especially her high cheekbones, an almost flat Habsburg jaw suggested something more sinister, perhaps the occurrence of a cousin marriage in the past generation or two.

Zeno handed us each a mug of steaming mint tea and went back to poke the fire. He took hold of a hookah and started dissecting it. He beheaded it first and put a lump of brown jaggery sugar in the neck of the *chillum* filling the rest of that narrow tunnel with tobacco, herbs and embers. The room filled with the sweet whiffs of the herbs. Zeno held the serpentine hose of the said apparatus in his hand and taking the wooden mouthpiece between his lips, closed his eyes and took a deep, satisfying drag. I felt that serene expression on his face soothing my own soul and the elixiric smoke filling my own lungs. Having verified the strength and quality of the tobacco, he passed the hose to me, which I accepted with utmost delight and after inhaling my fair share of the soul-nourishing smoke, I passed the hose to the Goth, who started sucking the life out of the grumbling pipe. After a few deep puffs, she started speaking again peeping inside the mouth of the limp hose as if trying to find something in it.

'Knee is the new cleavage,' she said. 'You may have heard the phrase. This is a belief dearly upheld in my little village amongst the aesthetes and loafers alike. My village Zanuia – famous for its sugarcane, amulets and gonatophiles – is located in the land of Lahnda[1] and at the distance of a day and a night on a carriage with a hardy steed from the ancient city of East Phalia (not to be confused with its more famous western counterpart in Germany). It is an anomaly of the modern age where the Internet and horse carts exist side by side without hurting each other. People of my village are hardworking, hairy and superstitious. They are proud of their traditions, the most prominent one amongst which is the covering of the entire female body under specially designed tents or curtains to save it from being rusted by the elements of nature. This tradition is by no means limited or unique to our region, as you must know. There are many other lands where a female child is covered under heavy sheets right after her birth. However, what makes this custom as practised in our village unique is that a gap or cavity is cut in the sartorial tent around knees. Perhaps, originally this hole was meant as an inlet or outlet of air. However, thanks to some daring rebels who liked to bend rules and knees and would reveal what's more than necessary from the health point of view, this hole has turned into the centre of fashion for the village women. Trends in the mode, fashion, fetishes and perversions revolve around the knees. On the occasion of marriages, parents of a young woman send pictures of their daughters' knees instead of her face, which cannot be revealed to an unknown man, to the prospective suitors. Stylish wenches and coquettish lasses apply all kinds of rouges and powders to these joints. They whet their knees to make them glossy in order to attract the gaze of the others. Needless to add that yours truly could boast of having a great fashion sense when it comes to *les genoux*. Not that the rest of the body is left uncared and unkempt to rot under the curtains. I remember my Amma used to put a combination of antimony and rosewater in my eyes to make them look bigger and darker. On some special occasions, I would even be allowed to wear some eyeliner and fake eyelashes. Now I think how pointless all that was when nobody could see my eyes but, erm, I haven't yet introduced myself.

'I, Leila Zanuzan, was the only child of my parents. Thanks in large measures to my father's abilities in the supernatural and an old wrinkly vellum, my family had the status of the local sovereigns. This parchment, allegedly made of dried yak skin and hanging from the ceiling of my father's clinic, traced my family's lineage all the way back to Genghis the Great Mongol, to whom most of the Asiatic worthies owe their bloodlines, on one side (the front) and to Merlin the sorcerer on the backside. The oral legend circulating around the village, however, added that our family was

---

1. The name of this region literally means 'going down' or 'descending' and has come to signify 'the place where the sun sets' or in short 'the west'. Mecca is also known as Lahnda in the local languages, and lying with one's feet towards the Lahnda is deemed sacrilegious. Multan, the principal city of the region, is known as 'the City of Dead Saints'. According to an Urdu saying: پدر اگر و اگر دلی مگر ملتان سب کا Agrā agar, Dilli magar, Multan sab kā padar 'Agra and Delhi are only ifs and buts, Multan is the father of all'.

the progeny of a quadruped couple found in Noah's ark. Although slightly hard to believe, this myth obviously added to the dignity and glory of our family.'

Leila spoke Urdu and Persian with the *legato* and broad accent of the plains between the rivers Hydaspes and Acesines, with shorter vowels and less sharp consonants than the way they are pronounced further west. It reminded me of a jug brimming with refreshing, salty *lassi* and the way some Indus valley *kāfi* singers sing Amir Khusro. People of this region are known for their peaceful and hospitable nature.

'My Baba was officially known as the Grand Compounder by his reverent clients,' she continued. 'He had acquired a degree in pharmacy and necromancy from a famous university and, as I said earlier, nature had been generous to him in bestowing upon him the gift of clairvoyance. He was, moreover, the best amulet-writer in the entire country. His charms were renowned to perform miracles, to help you grab your unruly dreams by their horns and muzzles. Whether to cure you of incurable maladies, reignite the flame of love in the faithless belly of your skirt-chasing husband or your cuckolding wife or to burn down the granary of your rival stock-hoarder, his amulets had never failed their magic. He was also famous for his skills in interpreting the omens, signs and dreams. Scores and scores of worthies, ministers, celebrities and courtiers visited him every day seeking his help and guidance in interpreting various symbols of their dream worlds. But he was particularly popular amongst that indefatigable tribe of men variously known as harassers and stalkers of women and famous for their tenacity, who would benefit greatly from his organic and gluten-free love potions.

'Every morning a long queue of his clients, each holding a phial of their fresh urine waited outside the closed gates of our huge mansion. At 08:33 sharp —Baba had been advised to start work at that auspicious hour by the Super-Superstitioner of the State – the first visitor would be allowed to enter and kiss my

Baba's hands. Whilst he would continue telling his worry beads, the supplicant, without needing to say a word, would merely bring the phial of his urine to Baba's attention. Then Baba, may his soul rest in peace, would shake the phial, look into it, smell it and diagnose the ailment of the diseased or divine the future of the supplicant. He would scribble something in an illegible script, supposedly in the hand of djinns of the desert, on a small piece of paper and hand it to the troubled person. There were various ways to use this chit of paper depending on the ailment and predicament of the supplicant. If, for instance, he had a cancerous growth causing him pain in his body and mind, he was to boil the paper in water and drink it three times a day. If, on the other hand, his problems were caused by another, say a bonnie lass indifferent to his harassing texts or an annoying political rival, the seeker was to find a way to add a few drops of the boiled charm water in the morning tea or coffee of the said lass or the politico and wait for them to fall in love with him or fail in the election. Sometimes, albeit rarely, these charms would end up in unpredictable places and produce the strangest results.

'Despite being perfectly aware of the gravity of his work and the responsibilities it carried, Baba was not completely devoid of humour. I remember once two young lads carried in a third youth in a palanquin who looked exceedingly pale, showing all signs of a jaundiced liver or excessive consumption of illicitly distilled spirits or even melancholy caused by unrequited love. One of the lads kissed Baba's hand and handed him the phial of the sickly youth's urine. Baba brought his nose to the phial for a brief second, handed it back and said, "Nothing to be worried about. He has consumed more mice than his normal intake but seeing his young age of four years and robust constitution, he should defecate them out in a day or two". Having listened to this enigmatic speech, the pale youth jumped out of the palanquin, kissed Baba's feet and admitted that the phial was filled with cat's piss and it was meant to be an innocent practical joke. Baba's lips distorted to sketch a faint smile, while with a gesture of his hand, he stopped his servants who wanted to thrash the excrement out of these devilish youngsters. Baba also wrote on a chit of paper in his djinnish script for the gluttonous *Felis catus*.

'Thanks to Baba's skills at supernatural, we had come to increase the size of our lands and herds of horned kine and horny oxen. Like the men of my family, our cattle had an unlimited freedom to graze wherever they liked. When our bulls, *Bos taurus*, wandered out to a serf's cotton fields, they were left to graze freely, without being least perturbed – no one could harm anything belonging to us. I grew up seeing arrays of servants bowing and kneeling, waiting to obey the wishes and commands of my family members. Women from the village came to cook for us. Their men ploughed our fields before taking care of their own crops.

'In short, we had everything one could wish for and yet despite all that Baba did not seem happy. I cannot say that he didn't love me but his behaviour to me can be best described as contradictory. At times, I would catch a glint of smile in one of his eyes while its twin would be brimming with tears. I did not understand the cause of this perplexing behaviour but whenever I asked him why and how he was both smiling and crying at the same time, he would reply in his succinct way, "My little mole, you'll understand it one day when you have daughters of your own." He used to call me his little mole back then, by which he meant *Talpa caucasica*.

'In those days of my childhood, which feel so remote now, the natural beauty of the village had not yet been marred by the onslaught of the civilisation. Life was simple and revolved around the few basic necessities. Baba had valiantly forestalled the state's efforts to construct a school in the village on many occasions. Thanks to his abilities to foresee the future, he had warned the good-hearted people of the village of the harms of schools and education. He had told them that sitting in lecture halls for long hours could turn their boys into sissies and their girls into tomboys and reverse the natural order willed by tradition and values. People listened to his wise words and thrashed any state employees who would venture there every few years to survey the lands for the construction of a school. I, however, was taught to read and write and count and tell the time by an old, distant uncle, who looked more like a dried date than a man.

'The village was encircled by vast and thick fields of sugarcane, *Saccharum barberi*, the principal crop of our region, which provided a livelihood for most people. These dense fields served as a barrier between the village and the rest of the world out there, an ideal meeting place for romantic or adulterous couples, a refuge for the exotic fauna, mainly wild boar and above all, a vast open-air lavatory. Having lavatories at home was still an exotic, and for some, an unhealthy idea. The more superstitious even thought that little bog creatures came out of the toilet hole to drag you to the netherworld. Apart from my own household, it was only two other landowning families, who had dared to build an out-house for their usage. The rest of the villagers had to go to the sugarcane fields to answer the various calls of nature. Womenfolk, as a rule, visited the fields in a large group in the evening to perform their daily necessities. However, the mass pilgrimage in the evensong to the sugarcane fields served more than the obvious purpose. Women would gather there to exchange their take on the current affairs, converse on the state of that year's crops, learn to play flutes, compose *māhiyas*[2] and relate smutty jokes. In the unwritten book of the village customs, these fields had the status of a sanctuary and women were allowed to shed their sartorial layers once they reached there.

---

2 The vocative form of *māhi* 'beloved', probably from Persian *māh* 'moon'. Here meaning, a vernacular couplet with simple themes and with lines always ending at this word. An example of a typical *māhiya* in Shahpuri and English:

> *Sāvi sar māhiya*
> *I'm not coming, you wait na kar māhiya*

('Reeds are green, o beloved – I'm not coming, don't wait, o beloved').

'For the children of the village accompanying the older women in the evening to their business these fields provided another attraction. The village carpenter, a kind and childless widower, had constructed a theme park there. It wasn't a very sophisticated affair but there were swings of many kinds tied to the high and robust branches of plain and oak trees where the children spent the time of their lives swinging and singing in the air. I, however, was not allowed to go to this magical swingland or mingle with the children of the *kammi-kameen* or riff-raff, as my mother called them.

'I didn't have any cousins. None of Baba's many brothers were married, being content with buying the fresh milk from the market instead of having the nuisance of keeping a buffalo, a *Bubalus bubalis*, at home, as they'd proudly say. And I'd have spent an utterly lonely childhood, had my mother's head not been invaded by lice one summer, or rather had she not developed an extremely sweet tooth out of the blue, or in fact, had she not dreamt one night that she had lost her pancreas.'

Mrs Kennedy
and the Camel-man

'I RECALL THAT NIGHT VIVIDLY,' Leila continued. 'Amma had woken up in the middle of the night screaming her head off. I rushed to her bedroom to find Baba scolding, threatening and shaking her frantically. But she wouldn't stop screaming. When she had screamed for a good half an hour or so, he seemed to remember an ancient trick. He brought Amma's slippers near her nose and the magical smell brought her back to her senses. After a brief pause she said, "Someone just came to my bed. I couldn't see her face because she was wearing a cloak. She put her hand here". She pointed to her stomach. "She took my pancreas out of my body, hid it somewhere in this room and went away. I could not stir or do anything to stop her because I was scared to death". Baba thought it was an absolutely preposterous idea and told her to come to her senses. "Your pancreas is not located where you're pointing at," he said. But Amma was adamant. "She took my pancreas away but it's still somewhere here. Right in this room," she kept repeating in a hysteric way. Finally, Baba gave in. He called the maids and asked them to look under the carpets and in the chests that had not been opened in ages. Of course, there was nothing out of the ordinary there. He told Amma to go to sleep. "No, I cannot sleep," she whined. "I want to eat something sweet. Bring me some *halva*." And that was the beginning of Amma's obsession with puddings and sweetmeats.

'She would gather heaps of sweets and puddings from across the world around her every morning and while some village maiden would be fanning her in the courtyard, she would be wolfing down various sweetmeats – Multani *sohan*, Dehlavi *qalaqand*, Khushabi *dhoda*, Shahpuri *patisa*, Gaziantep *baklava*, Bengali *rosho-gulla*, Yorkshire parkin, Isfahani *gaz*, Occitan nougat, Florida key lime pie, Mesopotamian *carasucia*, Manila *halo-halo*, Eton mess – throughout the day. She seemed to have no control over it. When Baba hid her sweets sometimes out of annoyance, she would go out in the sugarcane fields and would suck the sap out of the ripe canes. Now, as you can imagine, gradually this sugary gluttony had resulted in her blood turning abnormally sweet – so sweet that she became a favourite of all kinds of blood-sucking vermin and parasites – mosquitoes, fleas, bedbugs, midges, you name it.

'One morning, she woke up with an excessively itchy head and the more she scratched it, the more unbearable it became. She realised with horror that her head had been infested with a large colony of lice, *Pediculus humanus capitis*. She ran to the bathroom and washed it with oils, soaps and shampoos but the stubborn lice would not leave her. She told Baba about it, who told her off. "I saw it coming. Your blood has turned sweet. What do you want me to do now?" Nevertheless, he gave her an amulet to hang around her neck but that was just as futile. Meanwhile the itch had become agonising.

'Amma had no choice now. She had to get the insects exterminated one by one. She sat down in front of the mirror and tried to get hold of the bloodsuckers in her head but soon realised how difficult it was to find the agile vampires. So far, she had been too proud to let her maids know that she, like a homeless urchin, was providing food and shelter to insects but seeing that she, herself, was totally helpless before the vermin, she had to think of other options. An alternative was to get her head shaven but that would have caused a lot of rumours and a greater embarrassment.

Nevertheless, when she finally swallowed her pride and appointed her maids to the task, the wretched lice proved equally elusive for them. They would dodge their chasing fingers easily. That's when Zara's mother, Asala, brought her daughter to our courtyard.

' "Your excellency, my little one has an extremely sharp pair of eyes," Asala said proudly. "She is very good with lice and every time the darned crawlers visit my head, she gets rid of them for me". Amma looked at the puny child in disbelief but seeing no other option, squatted down helplessly with her back towards Zara the Delouser, who sat above my mother's head to have a better look over it and in this temporary higher position, found lice in the dark folds of my mother's hair, caught the fleeing thief, placed it on the nail of her left thumb, using its right counterpart to crush it. Amma's head was clean in a couple of hours.

'After that day Zara became a regular visitor to our house and owing to the same number of years that we'd been in this world, we became good friends. She was a child of joy, always dancing and prancing about and infecting everyone who came in her presence with the joy of life. A skilful impersonator, she could mimic and imitate various animals and celebrities in such an effortless way you would never be able to differentiate between the two kinds. Had she been born in a different milieu, she might have become a great voice artist. But unfortunately for her, she was born in a backward village in a Mirassi family. Amma appointed her as my official playmate, which meant that her parents were paid to let their daughter play with me. We had the best toys, puppets, catapults and slingshots at our disposal but I felt that she didn't find it very exciting. "Don't you like playing with me?" I asked her one day.

' "It's not that. It's just that since my parents have started making me come here, I can't go swinging."

' "And what's so good about those swings in the field? It stinks there. Anyway, I can ask anyone to get a swing built in our own courtyard, if you can't live without one."

' "You have to see the swingland for yourself. All the children of the village go there to play. Here it's just you and me." She told me so many enchanting stories of the swingland and the fields and all the amazing rides and swings out there that soon I was dying to be there too and see everything with my own eyes. It took me many days to persuade Amma, who finally gave in on the condition that I would be accompanied by a retinue of guards and would speak to no one in the playground except Zara, lest my language should get polluted by the common vocabulary.

'I remember the evening we went together to the fields. It was my first encounter with the village children. Once our *yakka* or one-horse carriage reached the sanctuary of the field, I took off my curtains, revealing the latest fashion from the city – a starched dress with a flowery pattern with my hair neatly tied in Dutch braids. All the children came running towards me. "Is she a fairy?" "No, she is a talking doll from the Qaf mountain." "She's made of China." "No, of crystal." I heard them whisper in each other's ears. Some wanted to touch me but were put off by the stern faces of my guards. One dared to speak, "Would you like us to swing you?"

' "Tell them that I'd like that," I asked Zara to be my intermediary.

' "She says she'd like that," she repeated my words.

'The swingland was as fabulous as Zara's stories shad depicted it. Situated in an opening between the fields of sugarcane on one side and those of mustard on the other. It was spring and there was a yellow flowery shawl spread over the mustard fields. Girls of different ages were swinging high, their toes almost touching the sky, singing the traditional spring songs. "*Pilū pakiyān ni, ā chunūn ral yār*"[3] and "*Sakal ban phūl rahi sarson, koyal bole dār dār, aur gori karat singār*"[4]. Pilu is *Salvadora persica* and sarson *Brassica juncea*.

3 'Come, o friend, for pilu berries have ripened' (پیلو پکیاں نی، آ چنوں رل یار).
4 'Mustard is blooming everywhere, on every branch there is a cuckoo singing, and the fair maiden is adorning herself' (سکل بن پھول رہی سرسوں، کوئل بولے ڈار ڈار ،اور گوری کرت سنگار).

'Those were the best years of my life, playing and swinging with the village girls, listening to their songs, although for all that time I kept my word with Amma and never talked with anyone except Zara, who from that first evening onwards was my bridge with the village, my mouth to the villagers. For most people our friendship was extremely odd considering the polar opposite statuses of our two families. As I've mentioned earlier, she was a Mirassi. Amma had shown utmost lenience towards my playing with a Mirassi child. Perhaps some explanation would be helpful here. As you probably know *Homo sapiens* is classified into many orders and sub-orders in Lahnda and these classifications are defined by the profession that one's ancestors had chosen to survive in the bygone times. A strict structure of tradition and stereotypes has evolved around this pecking order. Below the feudal and clerical orders, which are obviously at the top of this hierarchy, are grouped various types of artisans involved in manual professions. Stereotypes assigned to each order make it easy to understand the behaviour of a certain group. Hence, for instance, a cobbler is always parsimonious, a barber always gregarious, beware the butcher for he is belligerent, and a weaver is always a numbskull and on top of that, not good with his numbers. The repertoire of local humour is replete with jokes explaining these traits.

'The Mirassis, whose ancestors chose to play music as profession, sit uncomfortably at the bottom of this hierarchy. The word *mirassi* is said to mean 'inheritor', a reminder of the musical inheritance of this tribe. However, the local populace prefers to call them by many pejorative terms such as *doon* or lowly and *kamin* or base. *Kanjer* or *Chengger*, which originally meant a jungle-dweller and now used to describe a necromancer or a third-rate illusionist, is the most commonly used term for the Mirassis and has gone beyond its meaning to signify anyone having the most tenuous links to any branch of the showbiz. I remember once watching a TV programme with my family about the expensive and glamorous lifestyle of the Gabor sisters. My uncles were not impressed. "*Kanjers* may well have money but what they lack is honour and you can't buy that," one said to the other disdainfully.

'In short, they are universally derided and loathed for their melodious vocation and the Mirassis of our village, a family of three, Zara, Asala and Miskin, the *pater familias* of the Mirassis, were not treated very differently. In the village assemblies, where Baba decided such important matters as the education of villagers' children, Miskin, always sat on the floor, universally ignored. He was dressed in the trumpeters' livery of fading red and green – and for this reason called *hinduana* or watermelon by malicious children of the village – throughout the year, with a grey turban, parts of which seemed to have been white at some point. Sometimes a mean-spirited youth would mockingly inquire about the regalia. "My grandfather wore this same uniform in the *Angrez* army, to tell you the truth," Miskin would reply with pride ignoring the sarcastic tone of the inquirer. He would also bring his shoulder close to let you touch the golden epaulettes with pride. "My grandfather blew trumpet in the army of the *Angrez*."

'Being well aware of the low place of musicians in the social hierarchical structure and to escape this derisory and scornful treatment, the Mirassis of Lahnda started moving west in the form of a mass migration in the eleventh and twelfth century. Blowing into their trumpets and beating their drums, they crossed Persia and reached the dominions of the Turkish Sultan, where *changger* turned into *çingene*, and which was further corrupted into *tzigan* or *zingaro* or *gitano* in various languages of their new homelands. If they were hoping to be treated any better in these colder climes, they must have been soon disillusioned, as we hear about the ill-treatment these brown tuba and horn players were given by their urban neighbours from the Balkans to Andalusia. They may have forgotten the traditions of their ancestral origins, but one can still find the colours of Lahnda in their gaudy outfits and their colourful language.

'It was my tenth year when perhaps to commemorate the mass migration of their ancestors, or maybe to escape the scornful attitudes of their fellow villagers, Miskin decided to move his family to the sea-port of G. One morning Zara ran in our court-yard panting. She said her parents had decided to leave the village and that she didn't want to move, leaving us all behind. She preferred swinging and running with me. She asked me to use my Baba's influence to dissuade her parents. I instantly ran to Baba's clinic, but he was busy with his clients, scribbling in micro-scopic djinnish hand. "Who are the Mirassis?" he asked without raising his head. Disappointed, I accompanied Zara to her home, where they were loading their tubas and horns on a bullock-cart. A crowd of onlookers with rubber-necks had gathered around them, without anyone coming forward to give them a hand. I felt sad for not being able to stop them but what could a ten-year-old girl do in that situation!

'I recall those lonely few years when the Mirassis were away. In Zara's absence, Amma withdrew her half-hearted permission for me to visit the swingland, forcing me to stay at home all the time. But besides my personal reasons, no weddings, birthdays, funerals, were the same without the tunes and melodies of Miskin's trumpet. Although nobody had noticed until then, the Mirassi family had been inconspicuously playing trumpets and oboes in the weddings of the poor and rich alike for many gener-ations. The other people of the village, however, missed them not for the tunes they produced but for the vacuum they had created by their migration. The simple-hearted people, who were constantly abused and humiliated by their social superiors, needed someone to target their abuse at and suddenly found themselves at a loss.

'After a few years of hardship, the Mirassi family found their footing in the busy city life. In order to sever all ties with their past, they had changed their family name to a more acceptable and less conspicuous: the Shahs. Perhaps Miskin hoped that like in the *Farangi* version of chess, where any pawn can elevate itself to the ranks of royalty when it reaches the final house, they had similarly ennobled themselves by settling at the last city of the land touching the sea. Mr Shah, who wanted to distance himself from anything akin to his previous profession, had found the position of a camel-driver at the local beach, where he would take the children of the urban citizens for a ride on this exotic creature, *Camelus dromedarius*. Later, when I once inquired him why he had chosen such an unconventional career, he described a certain Bashir Ahmed as his role model. He explained that this Bashir Ahmed was the best dromedary-driver in the city of Caracci (the C-port) when the then first lady of the US of A came there on a state visit.

' "Her name was Jackie, to tell you the truth, or Jeanie, I can't remember now but what I remember is that she was the Queen of America, where Rambo lives," he liked to tell this story with excitement. "And she was so beautiful that when they gave her a glass of pomegranate juice, you could see the red fluid passing through her transparent skin, why tell the lie. Not that I was there to see this. I only heard this from someone who had once been to Caracci. So, she went on a camel ride with Bashir, to tell you the truth, and what happened then, everybody knows." I would shake my head to show my ignorance at the events that subsequently transpired, which would slightly annoy him every time he told me the story.

' "What? You don't know?" he would say with a touch of impatience. "And I thought you were educated. So Bashir impressed the *Angrez* lady with, erm, how manly he was and how skilful and how he could stand on the camel's back and sing serenades and this all impressed Mrs What'shername, to tell you the truth, and she got him and his camel a visa each to come to America where he became the special camel driver of their King.

And that's why I too chose to be a camel-driver, you see. To take *Angrez* ladies on the drive of their lives, why tell a lie."

'Miskin waited for five years for a Jacqueline to ride his camel and invite him to the new world. In the end, he lost all hopes to ever see any *Angrez* or *rangrez* woman. He was standing on the forked road of dilemmas not knowing whether he should carry on as the camel-man or try his luck in some other profession, when Baba came to his rescue. There are two versions of the story as to why Baba was strolling on the beach that day. According to his own account, he had been invited by a special client to G. and had walked down to the beach with his retinue after the appointment. Amma, on the other hand, claimed that she had found out that it was one of Baba's mistresses, who'd had a sudden whim to ride on a humped creature.

'However, both versions of the story agreed that it was on the beach that Miskin, or Mr Shah, met Baba. As soon as he saw Baba, both the love of his village and memories of his childhood, which were sufficiently distant to have acquired a new rosy glow, were rekindled in his heart. He ran to kiss the hem of Baba's shirt. Baba, on the other hand and despite his psychic abilities, was unsure of the identity of either the man or his camel. Whilst Miskin was introducing himself and proudly explaining how he had managed to ascend the property ladder and that his only daughter had been studying in a school, Baba attentively listened to him to the astonishment of his entire retinue and as soon as the ex-musician finished his self-laudatory speech, Baba offered him a proposal.

' "*Meschino*, the position of the village baker is vacant. How much do you earn here? Am I wrong to imagine that you make around 60 d. on a sunny day?"

' "Once I made 72 d. in one day, your excellency."

' "I am willing to pay you 80 d. a day from my own pocket and you can obviously keep the earnings of your sales."

'This extremely generous proposal was met with astonishment

from the entire company. Miskin stood there with his jaws left ajar, not knowing what to say. Taking his bewilderment as a sign of hesitation, Baba increased the reward.

' "Your family will also be allowed to play music on the full moon nights outside the sugarcane fields."

'Miskin kissed Baba's hands in gratitude and accepted the offer instantly. The musical family was back in the village in a few days. One day, Baba's favourite fool ventured to ask him about this enigmatic offer.

' "Sire, may you prosper for eternity, you have hundreds of men and beasts at your service. Why, if I may ask, did you offer such a huge sum to a lowly trumpeter?"

' "You're but a real fool. Don't you remember he said his daughter was going to school in the city?"

' "Yes, sire," the fool mumbled.

' "She was getting all the wrong ideas in her head and if we hadn't laid a dyke on that stream, it could've turned into a flood. Could've turned nasty, awfully bad. What if the rotten apple had returned to the barrel to corrupt all the poor minds in the village."

'Blissfully ignorant of Baba's real motives, the Mirassis seemed to love their new profession. Asala was given the charge of the village bakery, which was in our case a *tandoor*, or a clay oven. This fiery furnace had been dug in the middle of a courtyard, which was adorned with a few wooden cots to accommodate the clientele. Here women of the entire village would assemble every evening bringing raw dough, which Asala would bake for a few pieces of copper or bronze. However, this was not the only attraction Asala's *tandoor* had for her customers. Thanks to Asala's humility and repute as a trustworthy secret-keeper, her *tandoor* soon became the social hub of our village, overtaking the sugarcane lavatory as the principal venue for villagers to meet and discuss matters, sign agreements or gossip on current and extramarital affairs. Every community needs a person who can be trusted with keeping secrets, without fearing the spilling of beans or the unsacking of the proverbial cat, and Asala was our village's unofficial guardian of confidences. Perhaps it was her expression-less face, which encouraged her visitors to whisper their private matters in her ear, or her assuring analogies. "My belly is like my oven. Your words will be safe there," she would say. And the secret-divulger wouldn't imagine that like the bread baked in her oven, their confidences could come out to haunt them. In short, a source of baked goods, news and gossip, Asala's *tandoor* would one day disgorge home-baked deities. But more on that later.

'I was happy to reunite with Zara, who had many interesting stories to recount about the big city and the odd people who inhabited it. Although her studies had been broken off suddenly thanks to Baba's generous offer, being a precocious child she had managed to learn a great deal in school in these three or four years. Baba hadn't realised that his offer had been a bit late or perhaps he could never imagine a child of such humble birth being as gifted as Zara. As I mentioned earlier, I had only been learning the more traditional subjects so far, she now offered to teach me calculus, trigonometry and algebra, opening a new world of x's and y's for me, for which I am still grateful to her. I also noticed that her vocabulary and mannerisms had been affected by the city ways. She wore her hair in a neat bob, bun or beehive, depending on the season of the year and talked about swashbuckling film heroes who squinted their eyes to look impor-tant, glamorous heroines in bell-bottoms and with hoarse voices, and weather-beaten cricketers in white jerseys and red necker-chiefs. I found this change in her attitude a bit shocking at first but on a close scrutiny of my own thoughts and knees I realised that we both were adolescent now.

'Much had altered in the outward appearance of Zara's parents. Miskin had swapped his watermelon livery for a second-hand beige suit that he'd bought from a charity shop in G. after a great deal of haggling, he'd proudly tell me. Nonetheless, despite their audacious career hop from playing brass to feeding the entire village, in my family's eyes, the Mirassis never managed to fully wash off the stigma attached to the calling of their forebears and they were at best treated with a benevolent scorn. "You can keep a stick for a hundred years in a pond and yet, it will remain a stick and not turn into a crocodile," as one of Baba's favourite sayings went.

'Meanwhile, I noticed that the perplexing worried look in Baba's eyes fell on me even more intensely. Although I had been failing to grasp that it was I, the why and the wherefore of Baba's worries, I soon realised that he had been worried about my future, by which I mean my marriage. In my case, it wasn't as simple a matter as it sounds. That I didn't have kin to be married away to made my situation a bit delicate. Besides, in Baba's mind at least, traits like an inclination towards adultery ran in the blood. One of his favourite anecdotes was about a man who elopes with his beloved riding the beloved's mare. They have to cross a stream in the dark. The beloved's family are hot on their heels when the mare decides to sit in the middle. The man loses his wits with panic but the woman seems serene. "Her mother always sat in the middle of a stream. Give her a moment and she'll get up," she assures him. But this revelation seems to leave a mark on the man's mind, who pulls on the mare's reins. He is returning the woman to her clan. Why, you ask? Because he doesn't want his daughter to elope like her mother. Since the times of my great-aunt, whose shrine you can see outside the cemetery, our clan had to be very careful with daughters and their suitors.' The Gothic narrator paused here, probably to let this novel piece of information sink in her audience's minds. I realised now why her face had seemed familiar to me, also noticing that despite her close resemblance to the Lady of the Golden Nose, her face was devoid of that famous dimpled chin whilst her nose seemed quite ordinary and probably didn't have any miracles hidden in it.

She pressed the hookah hose between her teeth and mumbled

something inaudibly. Suddenly she looked completely worn out, as if this episode of her story was particularly painful to her or probably due to the tragic experience she had very recently undergone. Noticing this abrupt change in her appearance, Zeno hastily emptied the cot for her to lie down and concocted a fragrant beverage for her, which she gulped down slowly. Instead of lying on the cot, she stretched her legs on the rug and passed the hose to me.

Now while Leila is regaining her breath, let me take a pause in praise of hookah and make a confession. Amongst all sorts of pleasure equipment and joysticks out there, hookah is my tool of preference – everyone's best companion, loyal and suitable for all situations. You are lonely and don't have anyone to confide in, or maybe, it's not in your nature to trust people easily – just take your hookah to a quiet corner, close your eyes and inhale. It will listen to you and will give you wise phrases of advice. There's something noble and edifying about the way it keeps the contradictory elements of fire and water at such perplexing proximity. *Huqqa, qalyan, narguilé, argile, Karim Khan, lula,* hubble-bubble, pleasure-pipe – by whatever name we may call it, it's the first choice of all connoisseurs; men, women, caterpillars, princes and of course, lovers. An old Khurasani folksong is about such a lover who wishes to be a willow tree so he could be chopped and carved into a *qelyun* and thus have the fire of love in his head and the water of lust in his loins and that, in this way, he could entertain his *negār* ('beloved') someday with his gurgling belly and explore the depths of her soft cherry mouth with his hose.

After downing another glass of the herbal concoction, Leila resumed with refreshed energy. 'A few weeks prior to my fourteenth birthday, I had seen my mother directing the maids to clean and wash the furthest nooks and crannies of the house. I had also noticed servants looking at me and whispering indiscreetly. But that day, I woke up to find the whole house transformed. Thousands of people were running about, decorating the house.

I was quite excited, thinking all this commotion could be in preparation of a surprise birthday party.

'I was bathed in a tub of rosewater and milk. Honey was applied on my body to remove the all the hair whilst a paste made of turmeric and sandalwood was spread on my face to give it glow. Two skilful girls drew intricate patterns on my palms with henna. Finally, my knees were painted with a great deal of rouge and foundation. It suddenly dawned upon me that it was not an ordinary party. I remembered that these customs were related to weddings. This realisation was accompanied by a multitude of strong feelings. I felt angry and disappointed in my parents for having been so secretive. I was also consternated and uncertain about what was awaiting me. Besides, I wasn't prepared for the responsibilities of the conjugal life. I thought about raising my voice against my parents but felt too weak and indecisive. My mother, who had been scrutinising me closely all day, appeared to understand my situation and took me to a room.

' "Today is the most important day in your life," Amma embraced me and said with tears flowing freely from her eyes. "You'll never forget it for the rest of your days. In our land, every woman has to get married one day and leave her parents' house. I had once left my parents' home on the back of a rocking camel. Yes, it was an arranged marriage and yes, I had only seen the picture of your father, but I had fallen in love with the way he sported his starched eyebrows. They've gone so limp lately. I wish he still cared a bit. That day I was so happy to leave my childhood home and set off on that journey. My parents had spent extravagant amounts of money on the wedding. A Queen tribute band had performed on a moving carnival barge. '*Mamma mia, mamma mia,* let me go!' Your father was looking so dashing in his ironed striped shirt and kilt. He hasn't bothered about getting his clothes starched in a long time. His shirts are so limp these days. I wish he still cared a bit.

' "But you, my daughter, you don't have to worry about

anything. To avoid any unexpected calamities, we have an array of choices for the most desirable candidate for you, none of whom would have to take you anywhere. Your groom will live in this house with you." Saying this she departed leaving me baffled and frustrated. I was still furious at the fact that no one had ever mentioned before that day that I was to be married. At that moment, Zara entered the room. I didn't have to tell her anything. She read the fury and gloom in my eyes. I remember she had lately been condemning the marital institution, once summing up what post marital life entailed for a woman by a rather bold saying, which was so typical of her: '*diné chulla té râti lulla*'[5]. She held my hand and hugged me. I burst into tears. She wiped the tears off my face and said, "Hey, hey, what's all this about? It's not all doom and gloom. I know for us women it's an inevitable thing but as the saying goes, when one door is shut down, a thousand open in its place. Now, wipe those pearls off. I have a team of musicians waiting outside. We'll cheer you up."

'Somehow I found hope and courage in her words. "Whatever happens tomorrow, I'll get on with today and try to enjoy the damned affair," I thought. Zara brought a team of little girls, who started singing wedding songs to the beat of their drums and pitchers. Thanks to the Internet, their repertoire was not just limited to the local wedding songs. They sang in Turkish and Braj.

> "*Ağ elime mor kınalar yaktılar,*
> ('They put purple henna on my white palms')
> *qaderim yox, gurbet ele sattılar*
> ('Woe is me, they sold me away from home')
> *Oniki yaşımda gelin ettiler*"
> ('They made me a bride at twelve years of age')

And the Bride's Lament by Amir Khusro:

---

5 'Stove in the day and cock at night'.

"*Ham to, bābul, tore khūnte ki gayyā*"[6]
('We, o father, are kine tied to thy door')
"*Kāhe ko biyāhe bides*"[7]
('Why did you marry us away?')

'Their selection of songs, however, failed to brighten up my mood. Each song was invoking a feeling of sadness in me at the prospect of leaving my own home. Instead of cheering me up, they disheartened me. Memories of my childhood came swarming up. I finally made up my mind I wouldn't give in so easily.

'However, when a couple of hours later, Amma came back with half a dozen books in her arms for me to make a choice, I was strangely relieved. I realised the stratagems my sweet parents had been devising. They wanted to marry me off with a book so they didn't have to part with my share of lands. I can read the incredulous look in your eyes and as much as it sounds incredible, the custom of *haq-bakhsh*[8] or marriage with scriptures was common amongst the Lahnda aristocracy right until the end of the twentieth century. These feudal patricians were inordinately protective of their lands on which they relied as the source of their power and prestige. While sons ultimately caused the gradual division of estate to fewer and fewer acres, daughters were especially a bad omen since they could take away their part of inheritance to a rival feudal family and therefore, marriages within family were, and in some cases still are, considered a lesser evil. Otherwise, in a few generations you are left with nothing but a parchment proving your descent from a line of blue bloods but no lands to hold the falconry or jousting displays. Therefore, many *Arbabs* or *Reyis*[9] would marry their daughters to the Holy Book.

'Leaving me to choose my husband, she left the room. I looked at the selection of books. Baba loved to collect books written in

ہم تو بابل تورے کھونٹے کی گیاں 6
کاہے کو بیاہے بدیس 7
8 Literally 'forsaking of (one's) rights'
9 Titles of Lahnda and Sindhi aristocracy

foreign scripts to find inspiration for his amulets. Choosing one's husband is never easy but in my situation this process was made even harder by the volley of emotions attacking me. I can't say that I had overcome my anger. I finally realised what that contradictory look in Baba's eyes had meant whenever he saw me. They had always considered me a burden, a piece of their chattel. Besides, the way I had been treated all day was frustrating to say the least, being forcefully plucked and painted like a lamb before slaughter. Then I thought about the alternatives. A conservative husband made of real flesh and blood would certainly tighten the curtains around me and curtail my independence. A paper one could bizarrely be a better option in that situation. Therefore, when Amma came back, I silently handed her a very heavy and impressive encyclopaedia about the floral and faunal kingdoms, which I had chosen mainly because it was full of colourful illustrations. Amma was relieved. She hadn't expected me to give in so easily. She took the monstrosity from my hands and left with it for a makeover.

'At last, all rouged-up, dressed in a heavy scarlet shawl and embroidered harem trousers and decorated with baubles and tassels, I accompanied my tinsel-laden groom to a large hall in the house, which was brimming with famous people, men seasoned in the art of attending wedding ceremonies, victims of celebrity chefs and survivors of reality shows.

'The ceremony was a long and tedious one and when after several self-congratulatory speeches made by Baba it was finally announced that the dinner was ready, the announcement created a havoc in the hitherto civilised and benumbed assembly. Everyone started running amuck and in all directions, being hooked up to the smell of food. Mothers forgot their children; lovers forgot their beloveds. The entrance to the food hall was narrow and people started shoving and kicking each other to pass through the gates of heaven. A fight broke out. Many a man lost his limbs and manners there. It seemed like a rehearsal for the Doomsday.

'After the reception, I was taken to the nuptial chamber to wait for the arrival of my husband. Around midnight my mother came in holding my groom in her arms. She laid him on the flower-laden bed. I glanced at him blushingly. At least he was thick – so thick that you could use him as a dining chair. I touched his cover and found it velvety. I spent all night gaping at the pictures of owls and butterflies. It was a sort of escape – escape from the harsh and cruel world created by humans into the lap of nature, which seemed greener from that distant perspective. By the dawn break I had already memorised the Latin names of many species, genera and families. These artificial, unreal names enabled me to see the reality of this world in a different way. A plate of simple, boiled *Oryza sativa* gained an unfamiliar flavour and the salutary group howls of *Canis aureus* on full-moon nights took a novel meaning. In less esoteric terms I became more aware of the presence, in fact existence, of these other living members of our world. I developed an obsession of collecting facts about them. It was as if a door to an enchanted kingdom had opened up for me. I was especially attracted to the so-called anomalies of nature. Did you know, for instance, that the whiskered hens of Chile lay blue eggs during Lent or that the most painful sting in the nature is caused by coming into contact with a southern plant aptly named Suicide Berry because the unbearable pain makes you wish you were dead or that *butor* is a wading bird that can both moo like a bovine and write essays on Baudelaire or that the regular exposure to the noise produced by a screaming willow is the remedy for over fifty physical ailments including premature baldness in human babies?

'Days and nights relentlessly followed each other to unroll the slow march of years. I wouldn't say that I was actively seeking infidelity – in fact, I resisted the sudden pangs of infidelity with commendable self-control – but it was this very passion, thirst of knowledge that forced me to order more and more books on natural history. I took infinite pleasure sitting before the pile of my books, caressing their leather jackets, sniffing their greased pages every evening.

'It was during those days that I received an email from a stalker – a real stalker of flesh and blood. I think I still have it somewhere. Let me read it to you for I believe it will help you understand my story better. I can imagine that the likelihood of the existence of a village where people communicate with each other using the latest cyber technology and still abstain from having a toilet in their homes may sound astounding to you but that is Lahnda for you, a land of magical incongruities.'

A *Billet Doux* to a Comely Knee

L EILA FERRETED THROUGH various pockets of her cloak and eventually produced a yellow paper, which she went on to peruse in a solemn tone.

' "Pardon me for being so bold to take the liberty of writing to you directly. I assure you that I ruminated the thought many times before finally mustering up courage to pick up my plume. I am sharply aware of the enormous chasm between your lofty status and my lowly position. I know that you could, if you so wished, have me devoured alive by your hounds and yet I could not resist writing this humble missive to you – with a slim hope that you might find it charitable to listen to me.

' "As a way of introducing myself, I'm not one of your ordinary second-rate stalkers, who lurk about in the gloom like hyenas, timidly waiting for their prey. I am as bold as a billy goat in the realm of stalking. I have set down rules, written theses on this art, which remain unpublished at the moment. I have been hovering around the fields and stalking the *yakkas* and carriages of bints since I was a child and have seen millions of knees during my career but none, and let me repeat, *none like yours*. Allow me to laud the allure of your pointy knees, which have drilled their way through my heart, mind and soul.

' "In fact, I came to see your comely pair through a sheer accident. That day I had been riding on my bicycle for an hour or more after a *yakka* brimming with knees, hoping to be able to woo one or two when it managed to give me the dodge in the end disappearing in a busy thoroughfare. I was feeling down and dejected thinking the day had been ruined and was just about to go back home when, out of nowhere emerged your chariot with its musical bells jingling at the beat of your fair mare's content nods. I picked up my morale and started chasing you, completely unaware of where your musical carriage would take me. We travelled through the entire village. You had noticed my attention by then and if I'm not mistaken, my little minx, you kept giving me glimpses of your most charming jewels through the black embroidered tent you had donned that day. It kept me spellbound like a hound fixed on the whiff of a rabbit. I saw your marble knees peeping through your black burqa smiling and winking at me and I felt weak and watery in my own knees. I could imagine you to be smiling coquettishly under your heavy curtain. Ah, it was a pair of such dainty little knees with sharp features, milky in complexion with a hint of brown wrinkles covering the creamy layer. I decided to spend the rest of my years genuflecting in devotion before you.

' "The coach finally stopped in front of your castle. At first, seeing that it was the mansion of M. le Compounder, I was a bit daunted. I had heard the stories about how he dealt with people trespassing on his property, feeding them to his mad camels. But then you signalled to me with your lovely weapons of murder and I was fixed before your gates. I was savouring my eyes upon them when your coachman lashed me unconscious with his cruel whip. Before passing out with ecstasy and pain I could see your knees coming towards me, bending before my face and then disappearing inside your frightening castle.

' "A month has passed since the day I was first besotted by your knees and although, I have never seen your face, I know that the owner of such an exquisite pair of knees must have the face of a moon, pomegranates as breasts and feet made of velvety lotuses. After hesitating for so long, I have finally decided to write to you. I hope you will pardon my brazen chutzpah but I want to sing a serenade to your knees and become a slave to their charms. I shall be waiting for your response."

'Now I had no idea whatever he was rambling about, nor could I understand where the scoundrel had learnt to write or obtained my email address. I do not condone such behaviour but to tell you the truth, I was a bit flattered by the stalker's hackneyed words in praise of my γόνατα. I had moreover been bored out of my mind, so I decided to meet him. I read the letter to Zara, who thought he sounded like a right loco. I wrote him a line or two demanding him to reveal his identity. His reply came rushing back like an eager rabbit in my mailbox even before I had pressed the 'send' button and contained the scanned copies of his identity papers with account details. I pitied the wretched and summoned him to present himself the next morning under my window.

'As expected, I found him standing there wagging his tail with excitement, at the appointed hour. I opened the curtains of my window and let him have a long gaze upon my knees through the holes in my *shalvar*. He didn't look half bad, walking about on bendy legs which I supposed must have been the result of the long hours on his bicycle. I caressed my knees in a coquettish manner and he fainted on the ground foaming from his mouth.

'In his next message he thanked me profusely and repeated his wish to sell himself into my slavery. I had not known a man by then and he sounded like an amusing fellow. I was also curious about the possibilities an encounter with him might produce. In my reply I asked him to come to a secret garden to meet me.

'It was a breezy moon-lit night. I sat in a swing and let the breeze sway me with her gentle hands. I had gone through my wardrobe and chosen a ninja-style *burqa*, with a strip which tied on the forehead, a recent import from Najd, which was all the rage in those days. A bulbul, *Pycnonotus cafer humayuni*, was chirping in a branch and according to the ancients, complaining about the indifference of his rosy beloved. I waited there for hours but there was no sign of my mad stalker. At last, around midnight I decided to call it a day and returned home annoyed and frustrated.

'The next day I sat fixed before my screen waiting for his letter eagerly refreshing my browser every few seconds but apart from a few spam messages nothing entered my mailbox. This continued for many days. Gradually and painfully, I accepted the reality that the scum had made a fool of me and his empty words of slavish devotion were mere tricks to deceive me – but deceive me of what? I thought much about it in the next few months.

'The inexorable wheel of time kept spinning around its own axis, following its complacent habits, unconcerned with the human activity. I almost forgot about the stalker. Then one day Zara brought some tidings about him. She rushed in my room where I sat with my vacant eyes fixed at one of my bookish partners. Her face was pale and she was panting with excitement.

' "What's the matter with you? Have you seen a talking bird?" I asked her.

' "No, something far more exciting. A talking tree."

' "Yes, and I'm the Queen of Spades."

' "You may be the dog's grand-paw but I'm not jesting."

' "No, you're no Seinfeld. Don't say cheerio to your day job."

' "Will you listen to me for pity's sake? I saw him, it, no him. A tree that prattled like a parrot."

' "Have you lost your mind because you haven't slept with anyone for so long?"

' "I have been so excited that I did not sleep a wink last night. You remember that mad bicycle-man who used to hound your coach and harass you with his mad missives?"

' "Yes, how can I forget the lying bastard!"

' "Well, I saw him and he still remembers you."

' "Woman, what are you talking about?"

' "Last night I went to collect fuel-wood for our *tandoor*. I was chopping down some wood when I saw this extremely dry *neem* tree, just the kind of wood I was looking for. When I lifted my axe to chop it down, I swear I heard it whisper something to me in a human voice. At first, I thought it was the playful frolicking of the wind or a bird chirping an unheard song but then the tree uttered the same hollow sound louder and louder. I paid attention to it and can you imagine what it said? It breathed out only one word: "Leila". I wouldn't lie, I was terrified at first but then I realised I had an axe in my hand. I gripped the handle firmly and convincing myself that it couldn't be anything but an illusion, I tried to hit the tree, but it called your name again. I knew there was no mistake about it. "Who are you? A tree or a man?" I asked him.

' "I was born as a man but now I am a tree".

' "O man of leaves and roots, what has turned you into a tree?"

' "Leila's love," he spoke in a dry husky voice. Feeling reassured by his reasonable replies, I asked him to explain himself.

' "My good woman, I pined for that beauty for ages until the day I lost all hope and went to seek guidance from her father who told me that standing motionlessly in a desert waiting for my beloved could help me win her heart. Therefore, I have been waiting here for all these months to turn into dust so that the wind may carry me to her. Like in those lines by Sa'di... "[10]

' "After hearing this I rushed back home but since it was very late I had to wait for the morning to tell you this".

'Hearing this strange news I felt both furious at the roguery of Baba and frustrated at the folly of this mad stalker. I was unable to comprehend how he could have lost hope when I was ready to grant him all his wishes and how he hadn't thought of having a normal conversation with the woman he claimed to love so much and how on earth he could have knelt before my own Baba to seek cure for his folly? I thought much about it but eventually I had to forgive the poor sod. He was just a flimsy marionette in the tradition's crafty hands. "Beware the woman's

10 امروز چه دانی تو که در آتش و ابم
چون خاک شوم، باد به گوشت برساند

mystery for she is as deep as the ocean and do not believe what she says for when she says nay, she means aye" and all that drivel, nonsense they pour down their throats about us, as if we women are mysterious creatures from fantastical lands. As if we are unable to speak our minds. I decided to punish my family by dishonouring their name. I asked Zara the whereabouts of the talking tree and went to look for him. He, the lonely *Azadirachta humana*, was standing motionlessly with his eyes shut. It took me some time before I could trace his features beneath the layers of dust and lichen.

' "Leila?" he said.

' "Yes, my mad lover, I am here to unite with you."

'Thick drops of gum seemed to emerge from his eyes. He said in a whisper full of sorrow that he was unable to perform the rituals of love as the sap of life in him had all but dried up. I told him that I had enough desire in my veins to boil his sap. The *Neem* tree is famous for its medicinal qualities, as you may know. Its bark can cure eczema. Its acrid leaves, when boiled with water, can be a remedy for diabetes. Twigs from its branches are used as a substitute for a synthetic toothbrush. Its roots dispel rodents and insects. Its bitterness is proverbial, and results from the toils and labours of love. We spent the entire night together in our long-awaited union although due to his shrivelled state, I had to take the more active part in the act of love. Our congress revived him, draining him of his pungency and soon the sap of life was running in his veins again. One more night in the arms of love and he would be a man of flesh and limbs. But the next night, when I went to see him, he was not there. My frustration knew no bounds at this second betrayal. I wandered until dawn in the desert in his quest but there was no trace, no sign of his existence on the forgetful sand. He seemed to have vanished as if he had only been a figment of my own imagination. The entire affair gave out the sour smell of mischief but before I could exert my faculties to delve deeper beneath its murky folds, something unexpected happened, bringing a mighty storm in the village and deflecting me from my undertaking.

'I recall the momentous day, which had risen like any other day at the orders of the fiery king of the skies, when a rival to the sovereignty of my family arose from the Mirassis' *tandoor*. I have already alluded to the ark and the great flood, which had once covered the entire surface of the earth long before man had learnt to fly. The tradition claims in its self-satisfied fashion that it was a clay oven, a tandoor, of a baker's wife in Kufa, whence the great flood had emerged to drown the humanity in its wanton and unprovoked fury, thus blaming the Kufids, bakers and ovens in one sweep. Since that day mankind has been advised to be cautious of these three evils but I believe my family had forgotten this advice.

'It was around midday when Asala came running into our courtyard, excited and gasping for breath with something round in her hands. On closer inspection I was able to make it out as an almost completely burnt *naan*. Once her excitement was slightly subdued, Asala claimed that while baking some bread for the rush hour at lunch, she had found a loaf stuck to the walls of her *tandoor* that was miraculously adorned with the secret and personal name of the Supreme Being. She displayed the said *naan* with pride. I remember the four brown horizontal lines, the first on the right longer than the others and the last on the left ending in a circular noose at the top. My mother, a wise woman, dismissed the bread as a mere superstition but could not stop her maids from leaving their chores aside to walk around the bread-holder in awe.

'Before long the fame of the divine *naan* spread to far and remote places. Thanks to the marvellous miracles of the Internet, memes, tweets, fleets, stories, posts, status updates, DMs, AMs, PMs, hashtags and gifs of the Mirassi's bread were going viral like COVID. And it did not stop at that. According to a common belief, any bread cooked in that oven would thenceforth acquire magical qualities and was believed to act as both a laxative and an effective cure for mild cases of Delhi belly. Many people from other villages and cities started swarming in throngs to visit the *naan* and paying large amounts of money to eat some bread cooked in the holy oven. In no time the Mirassis's house had turned into a shrine.

'Baba tried to show indifference to all this, considering it beneath his dignity to take superstitions entertained by plebs seriously. In the first Sabbath sermon he gave after the emergence of the holy bread, he talked about false gods and shrines in his typical humorous way. I remember the story he narrated on the loud-speaker of his clinic.

' "Once a man had an ungrateful slave, one of the meanest knaves you could cast your eyes upon. Whatever good the master did for him, the slave would not be happy and instead of paying his master's generosity with gratitude and loyalty, he stole money from him. But the master, although he was aware of the slave's misdeeds, was too kind to reprimand him for that. One day, when the master was away, the slave robbed him, loaded all the booty on his master's donkey and ran away. But he hadn't gone far when the donkey died of exhaustion in the middle of a desert. Unable to move any further, the thief suddenly felt sorry for the deceased. He dug a little hole in the sand and was mourning for his loss, when a passing caravan stopped there. The travellers were much moved by the look of grief on the man's face. Without requiring an explanation, they gave him some money and food and built a little shrine for what they believed was the man's dead relative.

' "Soon the fame of the shrine of a holy man spread far and beyond and visitors started bringing their offerings. The slave transformed himself into a respectable man, inventing a noble lineage for him and his donkey. The shrine business went well for a few years but then, as happens in such cases, another bigger and holier shrine sprouted out like a mushroom in another spot of the desert, eventually depriving the slave of most of his clientele. Seeing the source of his income being siphoned by this other shrine, our friend, the former slave fell into a deep depression. He was also curious to discover the secret of the new shrine himself. But what a surprise, dear friends, awaits him when he reaches this shrine. None other than his own ex-master was sitting pompously near the saintly decorated sarcophagus as the guardian of this holy place. The slave was much affected by the sight and approaching his master reverently, apologised for his past conduct and enquired about the holy person buried under the shrine. The former master graciously pardoned his slave and revealed the secret, "Don't be amazed. It's the holier mother of the holy ass that you'd borrowed from me."

'However, with the passage of time and success of the bread-shrine, Baba's self-confidence started to waver. His sermons negated the value of idols and superstitions. "Gods might be carved, sculpted and worshipped, but never baked," he reminded his listeners. The villagers were, however, not convinced. It is easier to worship the visible than an idea and bread is the god of hungry even if it is burnt and inedible.

'In a few months, however, the *tandoori* deity started decaying, thanks to the monsoons, which arrived punctually that year to help my family, but the blow had been struck, the foundations of our status had been shaken. The problem was not the bread but that it had chosen to be baked in a commoner's *tandoor* – a Mirassi's oven. Baba took this to his heart and fell seriously ill. He could not bear seeing his subjects fall into the chasms of the superstition. In his feverish delirium he kept raving about a bunch of Mirassis chasing him around hoisting burnt loaves of bread.

'As you can imagine, from the beginning of this scandal I had been banned from meeting Zara. She, however, had her own demons to face. Thanks to the publicity her family had accrued from the *naan* of miracles, many Mirassi families from the neighbouring villages had expressed their wishes to ask for her hand in marriage for their suitable and unsuitable bachelor or married sons. But for the first time the Mirassis had the luxury of choice. They deliberated over the matter for some time before deciding in favour of a boy from a blacksmith family. The date was fixed. Before Zara's wedding we managed to meet on the sly. She told me that Miskin had insisted that she, the daughter of a miraculous family, was too good to marry an ordinary trumpeter or a clarinet-player and therefore, had decided to hop one step higher on the slippery ladder of the social class by marrying her off into a family of blacksmiths. Zara, however, didn't seem too bothered about that. She had met her *fiancé* and said he was handsome in a classical manner, astonishingly well-educated and was working as a mason or an architect. She seemed to be over the moon and talked fondly of him. "I'll let you know how much of an ironman he is in bed," she said mischievously.

'I couldn't attend my friend's wedding. However, I sent some servants with presents for her. I heard the Mirassis spared no expenses on the ceremony. Miskin's trumpet, which he blew incessantly the whole day, for the last time in his life, could be heard in our castle. That night, after the bride had departed with her groom and all the guests had left, something unexpected happened. The Mirassi couple was found burnt in the same oven that had produced the blasphemous naan. The common explanation was that they had gone in the oven to find more sacred bread. No one still knows what really made them jump in that fiery furnace. The cremation of the family, however, could not stop the cult of the bread. Militant groups, like the notorious Society for the Protection of the Bread were formed who advocated that everyone should be prepared to die for the sanctity of the *naan*.

'Baba did not survive the Mirassis either and died the next morning. Just like the famous spirituals of the olden days that one rarely hears about now, he had predicted his own demise to the exact hour. That morning, after having been bed-stricken for a week, he gathered up some energy to walk to the parochial house, where the devout flocked around him to kiss his hands. Some of the villagers, thinking that it was a great opportunity to get their fates revealed, brought phials with freshly-filled urine. He felt irritated by the whiffs emerging from the supplicants' urine. Feeling indisposed to walk back, he asked for a palanquin to carry him back. He took his shoes off to get into the litter, as was his wont, and saw one of the shoes falling upside down, or on its face, as if it had been mocking the sky. He felt uneasy about this omen and asked the coolies to hurry. On the way, he halted at a samosa shop, where he had a stroke while eating *samosas*. "My last hour has arrived," he is believed to have muttered before passing out and he died before the hour was over.

'I remember that gloomy day. The sky was overcast. There were three funerals planned for that day. However, my eldest uncle, who took the family title after Baba's death, refused to bury the Mirassi couple in the village cemetery. "The death by fire is a sign of the divine wrath and we don't want to go against His will by giving these heathens a place in our village cemetery." I heard that Zara took the charred corpses of her parents to her husband's town.

'On that same eventful day, I realised that I had become pregnant. In fact, I had felt from time to time that something had been going on with my body, but I had ignored it mostly. My body had been giving me the usual warnings, but I had no reason to believe they could relate to a pregnancy. Then my belly started growing and becoming rounder and rounder like a taut balloon until one day when I realised I could place a cup of tea on it. My first reaction was of terror, as could be expected. I thought about the fate of all those poor unmarried mothers who had been punished for bringing a bastard child into the world. Once I was capable of thinking more reasonably after the initial shock, I decided to abort whatever was growing inside me. I started purchasing various devices for abortion on the Internet but anything coming to my room had to undergo a strict regime of controls imposed by my dear Amma, thanks to whom I never managed to get my hands on anything that I purchased. I kept dreading the moment my uncles would denounce me to the executioner, but that moment never came.

'When I was eight months pregnant, I realised that I could no longer keep it a secret and reluctantly decided to reveal the mystery of my transformed state to mother. I remember how scared I was before I mustered up the courage to utter the words, "Amma, I'm preg…"

' "I know, my daughter." Her calm and composed words left me shocked and speechless. Seeing that I was lost for words, she continued smugly.

' "I was not born in the last monsoon. Of course, my daughter, I noticed that long ago. We've made all the arrangements. You'll have an aquatic delivery in a warm pool – the latest invention of the crafty *Angrez* – and I assure you, you won't feel any pain. Everyone is having it these days. Back in my days the wretched midwives would kill you with pain. You were eleven pounds. I had to stay bed-ridden due to the tears and what not."

' "But, Amma, my…"

' "Yes, dearest, your husband is wild, isn't he? Do you think I don't know anything? I am sure you will have many more children," she winked at me knowingly.

'After that strange conversation I felt less frightened, although at the same time, I was rather uneasy. I didn't know what my mother actually knew about my condition. She could not have believed in earnest that I had been impregnated by a book.

'Before the fateful day arrived, Zara paid me a secret visit. She looked a ghost of her past cheerful, irreverent self. She told me how my uncles had murdered my arboreal lover the day after he had impregnated me. She said they had kept it a secret because they wanted to keep the honour of my family intact.

'This news shook the earth beneath my feet. I felt as if I myself had been murdered in my lover's place. I had been fed up with the hypocrisy of my family but now it was beyond what I could bear. Taking advantage of the throngs of visitors who were paying their condolences to my uncles and Amma, I decided to flee my home in my enlarged state. I followed the example of my great-aunt, thinking that the land, which gave her a shelter in her last days, could also provide me and my child a roof. Zara helped me to the train station in her husband's camouflaged jeep, which she was learning to drive then and therefore could not drive beyond a certain level of speed and driving at that tortoise speed, I was worried we would be caught any moment.

'As expected, the train was late. I kept pacing the platform anxiously, terrified of being seen by an acquaintance. Although almost completely hidden under the folds of my faithful curtain, I could still be identified from the distinctive features of my knees by an observant pair of eyes. I was also concerned about the baby. All that anxiety could not be good for it. For a moment I even regretted my decision to leave the relative comfort of my home but the mere idea of raising a child under that oppressive, stifling roof was unbearable to me. The die had been cast and there was no way going back now. Zara stayed loyally by my side, comforting me, distracting me with her keen observations on her new village and the bizarre customs of its inhabitants. "You won't believe this," she said, "the fashionable women there are meant to hide their knees and reveal their elbows and in Marsaglia to the north it's the armpits, which to tell you the truth, I find rather crass."

'At last the train arrived. The Devil's Steed, as it was called initially, was introduced along with other gifts of civilisation to Lahnda as to the rest of the former British colonies by our foreign masters, a feat of which their progeny is still very proud, as you may know. They never tire telling us how they brought us civilisation and built us railways. The natives, in their awe and reverence to the *vilayetis*, have tried to retain this miraculous invention as close to the original nineteenth-century model as humanly possible. This act of homage, although praiseworthy, renders the employment of these trains in any practical sense very difficult. Don't take me wrong. I'm hardy enough not to mind a few occasional jolts and jostles but the train I took that day with Zara's help was much more than just a few overcrowded and uncomfortable compartments. It arrived precisely three hours and twenty-five minutes and not a second later than its scheduled time. The staff members were dressed in the stripy red livery of the Raj days and were trying their level best to be generally rude. Every single passenger in my compartment, to my exception, was carrying a fowl – Partridge Leghorns, Red Junglefowl, Common Quail, all were present in their colourful regalia. For being the only passenger unaccompanied by a feathered friend, I was absolutely and universally ignored during most of the journey.

'At the last station before the frontier some armed and masked men entered our compartment. Without uttering a word, and after casting a brief look around, they randomly pointed the barrels of their home-made rifles at three of the passengers, two men and a quail. "Take off your tunics," one of the masked men grunted. The chosen ones doffed the required pieces of garments with trembling hands. "Let's look at your backs," the grunter poked his barrel in the ribs of one of the semi-nude men. Everyone in the carriage was holding his breath in anticipation. It took me a while to remember the reports of sectarian violence where men with marks of self-flagellation on their backs had been separated from crowds in similar situations and shot down for having inflicted pain on themselves, for some thought it offended their beliefs to inflict pain on yourself instead of others. In such instances, the marks of self-flagellation had been taken as the evidence of practising this offensive ritual and the judge, jury and executioner had decided then and there to impose their punishment on the misguided souls. Luckily for our fellow-passengers though, neither of them had any marks on their hirsute backs.

They were however forced to give up their seats for the masked men and had to remain standing for the rest of the journey.

'All this couldn't have lasted more than a few minutes and whilst this surreal episode was taking place right before my eyes, my body started reacting in another way. I started bleeding heavily. I got up to rush to the train lavatories. One of the masked men rose to his feet but noticing the pool of blood around me, sank back in his seat without uttering a sound. The body works miracles sometimes in unexpected ways. A couple of the poultry hands came to my assistance. Paying no attention to the guns and the masks and suddenly assuming confidence and authority, they ordered everyone out of the compartment. They held my legs, while a woman blew prayers in my face. It was a painful process but, in the end, I gave birth to a stillborn child.

'I remember having stared at the lifeless body for some time. I was left benumbed and didn't have a clue on what I was doing or what I was expected to do. I didn't cry. Not a single tear. The delivery had sucked out all the strength from my body. At last the train halted, jolting me out of that numbness. I made a decision then. I said farewell to my tent and wrapped it around the lifeless sapling child, who had moss for hair and branches for limbs. I had to bury it along with my past. I carried on walking somehow, my eyes fixed at the turrets of my grand-aunt's shrine, which seemed to beckon me here.

'Am I sad to lose my son? Well, he had been a part of my body for so long. But if not for my knees, I wouldn't have ended up here…' Leila fell quiet suddenly, busying herself with drumming some obscure tune on her knees with her long fingers.

Everyone was quiet for a while staring at their nails or following flowery patterns on the threadbare rug with bits of straws. The awkward silence had become insufferable and was hitting on our temples with tiny hammers that it had probably borrowed from the raindrops outside. The heavens were still sobbing pathetically.

A Saviour is Born

IPASSED THE PIPE to the foreigner, who took it with a low bow of his deplumed hat. The power was still out and if not for the flickering candlelight, Zeno's hut would be sunk in the dark. The silence was suddenly broken by our host, who got up saying, 'Forgive me. I forgot to serve you anything'. He brought a platter of nutty candies before us apologising for the meagreness of his hospitality. The foreigner muttered some inaudible formula to express his gratitude. Zeno nodded and taking a handful of candies from the platter, squatted down in a corner of the room and scattered a few lumps here and there.

'For rats and mice, so they spare my books,' he explained noticing our inquisitive glances.

'But what's the point in appeasing those little rascals, man? Why don't you keep a cat?' I asked.

'Or you could keep a mongoose, a *Herpestes edwardsi*. That could also keep the snakes away,' Leila gave her piece of advice, once again hinting at her exotic background.

'Terriers are very good for keeping rodents away and you know they're fiercely loyal too,' said the plumed man in a whiny voice. 'I myself once had one of those ratters – a cross between a Yorkshire and a Jack Russell. Quite an adorable fellow. In fact, I owe the discovery of my own history to that bundle of golden wires'. Then after a pause he added, 'Oh pardon me, I haven't introduced myself. I'm Freydoune but you can call me Freddy. My ancestors hailed from the ancient and most noble kingdom of Rey.'

I realised that Freddy spoke Persian with a thick foreign accent, pronouncing his 'l's dark and 'r's round (pronouncing Rey as something bordering on Whey) in the Anglo-Saxon fashion. Needless to say he couldn't pronounce his *qaf* properly, which is a flaw common in the speech of those of European extraction. If not for the unusual circumstances, I would have judged the *qaf*-less *Farangi* to be lacking any kind of morals, principles or beliefs by this incapacity but for some reason, I was feeling forgiving, almost overwhelmed by a fraternal love towards my companions and so, I will try to re-interpret his words to make them comprehensible to the good simple folks of Saqia.

'But before I move on to talk about my canine companion, let me provide some background,' Freddie said. 'In the twenty-fifth year of his atrocious reign, the Dragon-Chancellor Azdak, *Roy de Rey*, decreed the controversial order of vaccinating all male children against polio in the entire kingdom – an order that set off a series of riots and rebellions in Rey. You might have read that in history books. There are various theories behind the possible reasons for his passing this contentious law – the law that opened a box of catastrophes in the kingdom. Some maintained that it was just another step of blindly following the decadent Western ways, a tradition that had been going on in the kingdom for many years, though not without occasional opposition from its proud subjects. However, those in the know claimed that they had heard from the people in his intimate circle that Azdak, who had apparently been suffering with various paranoia about the imminent end of his rule, had dreamt one night about a five-point star urinating in the most insolent manner, with one of its hind legs raised, on the face of a sun burning with shame. Azdak consulted many famous dream-interpreters and soothsayers from around the world, including our worthy companion's noble father,' saying which, he bowed in Leila's direction, who returned the gesture with a slight nod of her head.

'These astrologers predicted the birth of a child in the

imminent future – now distant past – who would be responsible for Azdak's fall. Now, despite being a very cunning and wily modern-day ruler, Azdak nonetheless believed in the mysterious potency of dreams and had in past shown absolute belief in the soothsaying powers of M. Compounder. Therefore, he could not afford to neglect this very clear and portent sign. One thing that is a bit odd about this whole dream affair is the fact that he had presumed his power could only be overthrown by a male child – perhaps considering the way the star was urinating – and thus the law of vaccination was only limited to male children of the kingdom.

'Once again, the patriotic people of the land saw through the wiliness of their atrocious ruler and during the protest marches and rallies, the leaders of various dissident groups scientifically proved in public that the polio vaccine was in fact contaminated with poison. But I am running ahead of my story here, which in fact does not begin here either.

'My story starts with my accidental and pre-marital conception. My mother, then studying in a university in the West, had met and as they say 'hooked up' with my father on a fateful day. Sanobar Banu belonged to the first generation of youths from her country who had been sent abroad to study modern sciences. She had never before visited the little group of isles chosen by her Baba as the place where she was to study about tibia, humerus and sacrum and, as is customary in such situations, her first impressions were mainly to compare this floating land against the stability of home, *terra firma*. It rained constantly there showing no regard to the season of the year unlike back home where everything fit perfectly into its own season – a season of blossoming buds when the infinite fields of tulips raised their defiant red turbans as if they were afire, a season of torrential rains when the entire universe seemed to be purging itself, a season of falling golden leaves, a season of snow-laden domes – oh how she missed home! And let's be fair. She was so lonely. Her university classes hadn't started yet. She had tried to befriend some local specimens but what an ordeal! Years ago, in her school back home, she always topped her class in her English essays. She was proud to have learnt the language from reading bleak novels by Thomas Hardy and the sordid exploits of moody Byronic heroes but now that she was there, she was incapable of grasping a word of what the natives said to her in the street. "Aw-why? Aw-why?" Road workers in bright high-vis vests would shout at her. She felt so exasperated that she made up her mind once and for all. She was to go back home. She would not wait for the beginning of her classes. And once the decision was made, she started feeling better – a burden was lifted off her shoulders. She looked out of the window. It had stopped raining – the first time since she had arrived in this country or perhaps since the beginning of time. It was a sign, she thought, and like a helpless little bar of iron she felt being pulled by a strong magnet, summoning her outside.

'Once out in the streets she noticed how the world had changed. Everything seemed happy and limpid under a radiant sun, or perhaps it was she who was changing. The world was still the same. She noticed a radiant goldfinch perching on a sparsely clad birch and remembered how the road-workers had always smiled even when they greeted her with their unintelligible grunts. She looked around and found herself facing a cinema. She took that as another sign. The world was full of signs that day, scattered everywhere just to guide her. She walked to the ticket-office and was overjoyed when the few short phrases uttered by the clerk in black vest-jumper started making sense. She didn't pay attention to what was being shown and let the celestial benevolence which, she now strongly believed, had taken interest in her fate and helped her make this choice. With a ticket for the next show and the required amount of corn and soda, she found herself at the back of a dark hall.

'Not everything was going perfectly, however, as she soon

realised. The first few minutes of the film were enough to bore her to tears. The film was called *The Fallen* and was about a depressing man named Azazel with horns and hoofs like a billy goat, breaking into whinging monologues about weather, politics, fashion and women on every little occasion. Barely fifteen minutes into the film and the wretched goat-man had already infected Banu with his melancholy. In fact, she started feeling so depressed that she reconsidered her decision to stay in this foreign land. With these thoughts in her mind she was about to walk out of the hall when the entire building started to tremble.

'Hailing from a land well-acquainted with earthquakes, memories of the disasters these tremblings had caused in the cities of her native land came rushing into her mind. When the earth gets angry, when hills are set in motion. When your own shelter, your own roof comes down on your head. Feeble moans of men buried under debris of their own houses invaded her ears. And that great musician Bastami, whose golden voice had been silenced by his premature death during one of these tragedies. But she couldn't dwell on these grim recollections, which were suddenly pierced by the marching notes of a paso doble. The audience in the cinema started to stir in nervous expectation. Banu had never experienced an earthquake accompanied by a marching band before. She rushed to a *jalousie* and saw scores of uniformed men holding canes and rods and cudgels and placards, with many playing the march on their drum and brass and being led by an august looking specimen twirling his baton in the air and performing many tricks with it to the amazement of the gawking onlookers. The writings on the placards read, "Stop defiling Satanism, Yankees" and "We will not tolerate any blasphemy against Lord Iblis" and "#Jesuisiblis," "We will not tolerate" and "Death to this and death to that".

'Once the Satanists reached the entrance of the cinema, the band suddenly stopped its performance. The man with the banner made his baton disappear momentarily before producing it from his behind. He signalled to the band who started shouting slogans in the most organised fashion giving cue to the men armed with cudgels who started smashing the doors and windows of the cinema. After satisfying themselves with a good work of smashing and shattering, the mob continued its march towards the movie-halls. Banu looked around. Panicked members of audience were running about with the 3-D glasses still attached to their noses. Without fully grasping what was happening, she found herself lying under a row of seats.

'She could now hear men with canes hitting the glass panes of windows in the hall and chasing the bespectacled spectators. She heard some running steps approaching her hiding place and started slithering further and further, soon realising that she was not alone in her shelter. And that's how Banu met my father – hiding under the seats of a cinema hall. I can't say if it was love at first sight. I don't think even they could be certain of that because before they could see each other, they heard and felt each other's warm breaths on their necks. Angry steps were approaching their rows now. Banu's neighbour all but fell in her arms. She felt his body shaking frantically and grasped his tremulous hand tightly not knowing whether she meant to comfort him or herself by that gesture.

'Someone was shouting right above their lair now, "We won't allow them to make fun of famous people". Another voice shouted, "Let's set fire to this temple of blasphemy". But then a gruff voice, probably of their leader, blared, "Our work here is done. Let them think twice before they can mock another famous man. And now, let's move to the next cinema! Damn, I'm enjoying this. I have a horn between my legs."

"To the next cinema, ho!" Soon the shouts and slogans started dwindling in their force before finally disappearing from the cinema hall. As soon as our hiding couple realised that they were no more in danger, they fell in each other's embrace, probably enveloped by a shared feeling of escaping death. When they emerged from their shelter into the cinema-hall unusually lit with the broad daylight invading from the shattered window-panes and the cinema projector playing the end credits on the tune of Tchaikovsky's *Waltz of Flowers*, they found each other pleasing to the eye – he, a man with broad shoulders, athletic build and smiling kind eyes, she, a woman with charms, looks and dark ringlets – or that's how I imagine my parents at the occasion of their first meeting.

'Antoine Murat IX, my father, had appeared from nowhere, from beneath a row of red plush cinema seats to fill the lonely corners of Banu's canvas with the colourful hues of youthful joy. Since that day they were almost always together, learning to eat with chopsticks in the Japanese eateries, dancing free-style in the shady nightclubs of the centre, attending heated debates on the ever-changing political scenario of the Balkans. He invited her to the mountain home of his family and introduced her to his little wiry dog, whose descendent I was destined to inherit. There they both learnt mixing mind with the indigenous varieties of fungi and had an amazing time by the sound of it. After a month of courtship, Murat the ninth of his name, popped the ultimate question genuflecting before my surprised mother and was in his turn surprised after being told that it was my grandfather, and not the seemingly emancipated Banu, who had the ultimate power of decision. My father took a month's classes in the art of oriental etiquette, which he took for flattery, learning the distinction between *bande* (servant, the addressor) and *sarkar* (ruler, the addressee), before composing a verbose letter full of flowery metaphors and ornate expressions addressed to his future father-in-law.

'My grandfather was known as Qirmizi Bey, translating into Red Squire in English and Lal Beg in Urdu, due to his unusual, though completely natural, ginger mane. He was a morbidly traditional man and would never have consented to his daughter's marriage to a Frank, had he not been deceived by a silent letter in the old-fashioned orthography of the *Farangi* language. He was under the impression that my father's surname at the end of the long formal letter was related to one of the five Ottoman sultans of that name. Bey, who himself claimed to have some Turanian ancestry, was by all accounts brimming with excitement. "So what if he has the blood of the Safavid-slayers in his veins, he's still a Turk, although on the wrong side and misguided," he is reported to have said before writing in response to offer his assent.

'The wedding ceremony took place in Rey during which my grandfather found out the true pronunciation of my father's name. This apparently harmless piece of information proved too much of a shock for him and he died choking on a silent but deadly French *t* after gargling the *r* during the wedding dinner. The official post-mortem reports discovered that the fatal *t* had pierced his appendix.

'My parents had to prolong their stay in Rey to attend Bey's mourning rituals. During their visit Antoine had fallen in love with Rey, which he saw and imagined as the mysterious and mystical Orient and the mostly middle-class natives he met – dressed in western style and speaking his language – seemed to him more exciting and exotic than the snake-charming, rope-climbing, belly-gyrating, bucksheesh-schnorring, loin-clothed, kohl-eyed and swarthy native types of the Orientalist romances of a few centuries earlier. Fancying himself as one of Kipling's *Sahibs* amongst Flaubert's *Küçük Hanıms*, he decided to settle down to live the oriental dream. Moreover, the life there was mostly quiet and peaceful and although this peace was intermittently broken by public protests against Azdak's atrocious rule, these atrocities, however, had not so far affected the foreigners living there. Antoine bought himself a vineyard, a distillery, a dozen of native labourers and would have carried on leading a peaceful life, distilling the exquisite Shiraz, if not for the untimely passing of the infamous vaccination law that I've already alluded to. This time no one was exempted from the serpent's poison as the local populace called it. The entire nation stood up against this new blow on their values and traditions. The brave people opened fire on the vaccination teams, killed nurses and vaccinated the corpses with the venom they were allegedly pouring in the future of the nation. The conflict between the common people and the vaccination teams soon spread to the other walks of life turning into the failed but famous Vaccine Revolution.

'Foreigners had hitherto enjoyed the state's favouritism and had always been resented for this by most locals. First rumours and then reports of Mr So-and-So or M. Untel being hissed at in the streets or being asked to go back to their country, or being dubbed as fornicating aliens, started to circulate. Antoine, who believed himself to have a good deal of knowledge of the native behaviour and temperament, was still not discouraged by all this. Taking it as just another whimsical fancy entertained by the capricious indigenous populace, he carried on having rosy soirées with those broad-minded locals who'd confused socialising with westerners as the epitome of culture. He refused to leave his vineyards and shut his ears to the racialist hisses and yells.

'However, to her own amazement, my mother felt she could not – although she'd later claim in her diary she always wanted to – trust her own fellow countrymen anymore. She did not want to take any risks. She had heard tales of gruesome endings met by the local women who had dared to marry foreigners in other countries and times. There was no reason to believe such incidents wouldn't occur in Rey. The more she thought about it, the more it became evident to her that she had to leave her once beloved home – for my sake. Yes, this is where I enter the story.

'That day she'd decided to take the matters in her own hands. Antoine had spent another great evening at one of the famous cabarets of the city, *Kaj Kolah Khan*. A glance at Banu's clouded face was enough for him to realise what she was about to say. He gave her a long lecture pre-emptively on how wrong she was in mistrusting her own kind and how baseless the rumours were about foreigners being butchered in the city alleys. Unlike all the other times, when Antoine explained the world and life and all the big questions to Banu, that day she listened to him patiently and instead of saying a word in response, she grabbed his hand and placed it on her belly. I felt the tremor of my father's unsure hand seeping inside the cosy womb of my mother and mustering as much force as I could in my tiny foetal feet, delivered a substantial kick to the inner walls of my home. And if you don't take it as bragging, I strongly believe this one kick transformed my father. He jumped up with joy. Seeing that the iron was sizzling hot, Banu announced to the overjoyed Antoine that she did not want their child to lose her parents at the hands of her own compatriots or be envenomed by the pervert state organs. It didn't take long to convince him. He didn't think twice about the idyllic Orient before they boarded a private jet and came back to the peaceful West where children are not vaccinated with venom.

'I was brought up in the West without any knowledge of my origins or roots and of whatever I have narrated to you thus far. I was born on my father's estate in the north. My father, who had lost his vineyards but not the memories of his rosy soirées, spent most of his time in his library drinking on his own. My mother took all the responsibilities of the household. My parents, and especially my mother, never uttered a word about their past. Although they never said anything explicit about her roots, I was tacitly made to believe that they were a local couple. However, when I attained more understanding about my surroundings, especially after I was enrolled in a school, I started to see potholes in this version of their wordless story. For instance, my mother had a slow drawl in her accent and her mannerism which I had grown up seeing as normal was slightly different from that of the other women I saw around me, such as my schoolmates' mothers.

'Then my mother was obsessed with anything from the East, albeit in a slightly unexpected and perverse fashion. She had strictly forbidden everything least suggestive of the East in our home. Our food was devoid of sumac and turmeric. Our wardrobe had no pyjamas or cummerbunds. Even the names of objects remindful of the East were modified. Thus a carpet store nearby sold Freedom rugs on which, Freedom cats purred about luxuriantly – and God forbid that either would be permitted in our home!

'I had the zeal and curiosity of a Genoese sailor when I was first mastering the equestrian arts, taming my first bicycle, which I christened Durgut after a foolhardy Turkish admiral. I would set off exploring the little world around me, imagining myself discovering some unknown virgin lands. My mother would permit me to ride in all directions, save in the direction of the sunrise. East was the forbidden point in the compass of my child-hood.

'I studied in a renowned grammar school, distinguished for the quality of its Greek lectures, which I learnt avidly. I do not recall any particularly painful memories apart from a few times when someone in my school called me by a racialist slur, using names specified for the people of eastern origins. Although it was a very rare occasion, I found it harsh and unjust. After all, I was no freshie having arrived there hidden at the back of a lorry or a boat stinking of strong eastern odours. At the same time, however, these episodes would also make me more curious to know about my roots, whose discovery, as I may have mentioned before, I owe to a loyal friend of my teen days, a familiar lupine hound, whose fore-fathers and -mothers had served the Murats for many gener-ations. Many of my classmates entertained a morbid fear of canines and believed that the domesticated progeny of the once free-roaming wolves could forbid the angels of mercy from cross-ing the door and entering one's home, thus making it vulnerable to the onslaught of calamities and catastrophes. Nonetheless, I was very fond of this tail-wagger. He was one of those terriers, who were originally bred to catch rats in the north and are thus bestowed with wonderful noses. I had named him Γιατί because every time I talked to him, he would tilt his head sideways with the inquisitive look at his face suggestive of a long drawled 'whyyyyyy?'

'One day, while my mother was out and my father, who was supposed to keep an eye on me, had retired to his library to drink, I heard Γιατί scratching the hall floor and whining about in front of a large pottery kiln in a corner. I know some people might say he had felt some paranormal presence or spotted a ghost invisible from human eyes, but I knew the rascal very well. He must have smelt a rat, I thought, trying to ignore him but as he kept scratching the floor even more fiercely, I had to finally give in, if only to gain some peace of mind for myself.

'I got up to move the kiln, which my mother sometimes used to cook ceramic sheep and cows. The canine in the meanwhile was wagging his tail vigorously, probably hoping he would find some sort of treasure. The kiln was heavy and was stubbornly refusing to move. As soon as I managed to move it after long vigorous efforts, Γιατί started scratching the piece of carpet which emerged from under the kiln and which seemed to have lost its colour for having been buried under the heavy object. I realised the floor beneath it gave a hollow sound. I removed the carpet to find that there was a little door hidden under it. I opened the door and saw a staircase opening into a basement, just like in an adventure film.

'Like most children I had always dreamt of discovering hidden treasures in secret places and now I had one right there before my eyes. I wasted no time and realising that it was too dark down there, equipped myself with a torch and descended the staircase. You wouldn't believe what I found there. The walls of the basement were adorned with portraits of solemn looking men in luxurious oriental robes, their heads stuffed in impressive turbans. Several decorative items, which reminded me of the stories of Aladdin and Ali Baba's caves, were scattered about. There were magic lamps, flying carpets, turquoise and garnet rings, rosaries, worry-beads, cummerbunds, harem pyjamas, veils, sets of backgammon, mounds of *halva*, a platter adorned with the seven sibilant items all starting with an s as required by the tradition for the *Nouruz* celebrations, *divans* of forgotten poets, scimitars, barrels of petroleum, desert sand, dates, oases, mirages, jars of sumac and saffron, flasks of rose-water, beards, belly-dancers, calligraphic scrolls. In brief, everything considered oriental in the western imagination and its reproduction in the eastern fantasy was there. I spent a long while staring at these exotic objects, failing to understand their significance. I decided that I was going to hide my knowledge of this treasure from my parents, from the entire world in fact, until I discovered its secret. I also found a few diaries, which contained writings in a script then unknown to me, but which I assigned to be Arabic in my ignorance.

'I had a strange inkling that these diaries contained something significant about me, my past and my origins. I decided to steal the diaries in order to decipher the script. I sought help from the only Eastern boy in the class, who, having unsuccessfully attempted to decipher the cryptic sign declared that the additional dots on certain letters meant that the language used was not Arabic but *Ajamic*, a word signifying dumb, as I later discovered. After long laborious hours in the school library, I managed to learn the secret language and decode the diaries. What I read was most enlightening on my personal history. Everything from my mother's blues in the rainy isles to her encounter with my father, from his adventures in Rey to their return to the West was there. I surmised why my mother had always been reluctant to talk about her roots. I don't know whether it was the thought that I belonged to an exotic culture or just the rebellious urge common in children of my age to oppose their parents, but these discoveries kindled an obsession in me, an inextinguishable love for my real home, the land of which I had no memories. I started learning about its history, culture, geography, people, fauna and flora. I found out that the land of my dreams was still under the atrocious rule of Azdak. I learnt about the legend of his dream and the ensuing troubles over his policies, which had forced my parents to leave my homeland. The more I thought about it, the more I was convinced that it was evidently through my own hands that the well-known prophecy was to come true. After all, I was the only boy born in Rey during that month of dreams who had avoided the venomous vaccine. I was the boy in Azdak's dream, who was to urinate on his face one day.

'In the meantime, and when nobody was looking, I was preparing myself for my ultimate mission – to free my land from the atrocious regime of Azdak. I took a handful of judo classes but found them too demanding to continue after a month. Following similar results after taking up jujitsu, yoga and contemporary street dance, I decided that the physical fight was the weapon of the pawn, the cannon fodder of my future army and I, being the leader, was surely destined to lead my forces with my intellect. Therefore, I dabbled in telepathy and flirted with occult sciences for a month or two. I tried mind-reading with the help of do-it-yourself books, but the directions therein were too vague and in the end I could not make any sense or nonsense out of it. I remember sitting cross-legged for hours in a dark room staring at a candle, trying to imbibe some super-natural powers from it, whilst also attempting to ignore Γιατί's grumbles. I also followed Aleister Crowley and other occult figures on social media, but that fad too wore off eventually. After giving up on mind-reading and palmistry, I flirted with different types of rock bands. I joined the fan club of The Devil's Vomit, following their countrywide tour accompanied by rabid groupies and in the process somehow ended up popping my cherry. I got the map of Rey tattooed on my left bottom cheek and got my private jewels pierced after Prince Albert's fashion.

'The day after my eighteenth birthday I was suddenly filled by the realisation that thanks to all the skills I had hitherto mastered, I was ready to accomplish my destiny and march to my homeland. It came to me like a Technicolor daydream. I imagined myself leading my victorious army to Azdak's palace, whose henchmen ran around like headless chicken in the ensuing chaos. However, I was also bitterly aware that my mother would never allow me to travel anywhere remotely near the East and therefore the day after attaining my legal age at a public house, I decided to run away from home. As a staunch follower of tradition, I spent the entire night in the tavern downing pints of cloudy cider closely followed by shots of Mexican liqueur with fun-loving strangers to the health of my oppressed compatriots, who were surely unaware of my intentions and plans to be their saviour.

'I remember the foggy morning after that long hazy night when I finally left home to travel to the motherland, without disclosing my plans to my parents. I knew that they'd forgive me sooner or later. In fact, they would be exceedingly proud of me, I thought, when they learnt one day about the reasons I left home in such a way. The only true sad thing was to say υγίεια to Γιατί. He was quite an old fellow by now with grey whiskers and dim eyes and spent most of his time watching TV programmes about dog-whisperers. I saw him wagging his tale in a dream – perhaps about finding a rat or chasing a tennis ball. That memory still brings tears in my eyes.

'I had no clear idea of the practicalities of the path in front of me. My insufficient luggage contained a couple of guides about backpacking holidays in an Eastern country and how to survive the spices and Turkish-style lavatories, some pieces of light summer garb and a bunch of bananas to kill the effects of the terrible hangover hammering on my temples. My mouth felt like it was carved out of wood. My body was exhausted, my heart pumping hard, my liver trying to deal with the toxic matters in the blood stream and the brain trying to make some sense out of it.' At this point in his story, Freddy the Frank was caught by a sudden fit of cough, perhaps triggered by the memory of that remote hangover. Finding the opportunity that everyone perennially seeks to part with some advice, the gravedigger interposed in a know-it-all manner, 'Bananas? Well, my friend, why didn't you try some celery and mayonnaise? Though you shouldn't have mixed your drinks in the first place.'

'I've heard good things about mango pickle too and how it kills the effects of intoxicants,' Leila said in her exotic fashion whilst hastening to add, 'although I've never tried either myself.'

'Well, thanks but it's a bit too late knowing all that now,' the Frank continued his account, 'The only thing I was certain of was to keep walking towards east, opposite to the sun's journey. I knew that walking thus I would one day reach my destination. Looking back at that journey now, however, I cannot be so sure that I always managed to keep facing the orient. A compass would have been helpful. A sleeping bag, too. But despite all the hardships of the road I remember having stayed in an elated state. The thought of being finally independent and on my way to achieve my dream was reawakening the intoxicated state of the last night in my fevered mind.

'No one can, alas, run away from the bony embrace of reality for too long. After purchasing a few items of food, I had almost run out of the little money I had set off with. By the evening I was tired, hungry, feeling lost, and did not know where to spend the dark hours approaching this side of the world. In that moment of utter despair, I came across a poster on the wall of a tavern announcing that a caravan would be traveling in a few hours towards L., which was a major port and whence I could, I thought, embark on a voyage to the East.

'I rushed to the site of the caravan's departure and paid my fare with the few coins I had. We reached L. by midday. This city, the erstwhile navel of the financial world, still possessed the air of a huge market fair. Mercantile classes of diverse races and nationalities in their ethnic garbs were exchanging goods, trading their merchandise shouting their hawking rhymes in the language of the city flavoured by the salt of their native languages. I could discern between the Australians in flip-flops selling boomerangs, Hawaiians in florid leis hawking pizzas topped with pineapple in stalls shaped like canoes, Englishmen dropping their h's and swallowing their t's, while sousing their cods and chips with pungent vinegar, Pashtuns with majestic grey and white turbans with their beards dyed red selling snuff, fakirs from India in their loincloths exhibiting varieties of spices in myriad colours, their smells promising unknown flavours, Mandarin scribes writing notarised documents in the ancient calligraphic hand. A Scots-man was standing on a kerb-side blowing into kilted pipes whilst a bus-full of Japanese tourists, their faces covered with surgical masks, were being driven around various monuments of the city. The air was suffused with strange flavours and aromas. The magnificently decorated vitrines of high-end brands were exhibiting the enchanting seasonal outfits tailored by inventive designers and seamstresses and attired by bald mannequins with comely and proportionate figures.

'I was starving now and the smells and odours of the multi-ethnic cuisines were whetting my appetite. I could have willingly sold my soul for a handful of peanuts. I tried to carry on walking but my body could not bear the burden of hunger any more. Then, almost out of the blue, I saw a feathered burger of gigantic proportions approaching me. Convincing myself that it was merely my famished mind playing tricks with me, I walked away from him into the road, almost hitting an angry vehicle. I fainted in the middle of the road. I can't say how long I stayed uncon-scious but the first feeling I had after regaining my wits was that of being carried away from the honking muzzles of automobiles and cargo-laden carts in the soft arms of the burger-man before I lost my consciousness again.

One More Bird!

FREDDY LOOKED AT ALL OF US in a suspenseful way and downed his cold, mint tea in one quick sip. Zeno filled the cup with more steamy drink from the teapot. 'So, I was saying,' Freddy resumed. 'I was being carried by a fleecy, plump burgher, who distributed marketing and propaganda literature for a fried chicken-vending establishment, named 'Chicken R Us', as I discovered listening to the story of his life in my semi-conscious state. After hearing the plight of my homelessness in the few broken words I seem to have uttered, he took pity on me for some reason and promised to help me find a livelihood at his eatery.

' "It is true you do not earn the minimum wages but you can eat as many chicken wings as it pleases your tummy," he said. The words 'chicken wings' sounded like manna to my famished ears.

'It was past the busy lunchtime when the burger-man brought me into the chicken shop and only a couple of old-time gourmets were there dipping their limp chips in the gooey sanguine ketchup. The charitable burger-man seated me in a corner and brought me a platter of greasy chicken-wings. Having filled my stomach with the battered food and somewhat recovered my wits, I looked around and noticed her – or rather her milky globes. She was cleaning an enormous pile of small bones that the poultry-loving connoisseurs had left behind on a table in the corner. She was bending down with her back turned towards me and her faded denim seemed incapable to retain the ample and majestic derrière she was unwittingly demonstrating in the classic 'mason's posterior' pose. Baffled and not sure where else to look, my eyes were fixed on the tattooed paisley pattern on the small of her back, which seemed to be diving headlong with its sharp beak opening the deep crevice between her alabaster cheeks. I knew that I was besotted by that turquoise and grey paisley and the ravine it was dying in even before I had seen her face. In other words, I was under the influence of her buttocks before her other charms could enamour me. She turned around and I noticed another inked pattern on her bare arm.

' "I got it in Qazvin. They are exceptionally skilled with their *mina-khanis* there," she said in a matter of fact tone before rolling over the right leg of her trousers and proceeding to show me the upward journey of a crane, a haiku written in *Shekaste* or the famous broken script and an Irish lyre, adding that each was in remembrance of a journey or an affair. I stood there utterly speechless mesmerised by her abundant Rubens-esque pulchritude.

'Hugo, the burger-man, who had been lingering around in a vain attempt to shirk from his duties, introduced me to Vanessa 'Cunegondé' O'Shea. The story of my homelessness seemed to elicit pity from her too. She told me that the owner of the establishment was in fact looking for a batter-mixer and I just seemed to fit the role. She took me to the back of the restaurant where the kitchen was burning at an infernal temperature and where half a dozen sweaty chicken chefs and sous-chefs were engaged in various stages of transforming the dishevelled members of poultry into battered and spiced-up beauties.

' "One more bird!" her booming rhotic voice resonated through the kitchen, leaving me wondering whether she was announcing my entry or yelling an order to be prepared. After that announcement I didn't catch the glimpse of that ink-saturated beauty for the rest of the day, which I spent working in the resto's sinkhole till midnight without seeing the sunlight. I was asked to cover my face with a net supposed to prevent the chicken from being polluted by the odd hair that could escape my stubble. The head mixer taught me the fine art of mixing eggs into flour. I had lived in the luxury of my parents' home where I had never needed to learn anything related to cookery and so for most of that day I was totally clueless about the theory or rationale behind the act.

'Another worry hanging over my head like a sombre cloud that day was the haunting reality of being homeless, the thought of which kept pricking my mind persistently. I'd heard stories of how merchandisers of human organs kidnapped homeless people sleeping under bridges and the idea of losing my kidneys or testicles did not seem too attractive. I was still scraping my impractical mind for other possibilities when the hour of midnight struck and my colleagues started to leave one by one. I heard Vanessa's voice bidding adieu to the last customers. Half-realising that I must be free to leave too, I hesitantly left the kitchen to enter the dazzlingly lit main floor of the shop, where she was closing down the till, counting azure and green paper notes with impressive alacrity. Without saying a word, she signalled me to wait. I stood there observing the depiction of the city life on the walls through the framed photos by a photographer, who seemed to be obsessed with the blurring effects of moving lights. In the meanwhile, Hugo arrived muttering objectionable oaths under his breath. He had been attacked by a gang of vicious teenagers once again. The event, however, had taken place so many times that it did not seem to bother him much. He told me that Ness and he were squatting in a mansion in zone five, one of the outermost zones near the rim of the city, and I was welcome to join them. Needless to add that I jumped at the opportunity after muttering a few formalities. Things were working out finally, I thought.

'Ness, Hugo and I travelled through the overflowing intestines of the city, riding an underground serpent. The Baroque mansion of the squatters was a few paces away from the underground station and consisted of many empty rooms. As soon as I entered the building, I was attacked by the strong illegal fumes emitting from the nostrils of various delinquent occupants. Most of these turned out to be sons and daughters of grocers and burghers hailing from respectable middle-class families, whence they had escaped in a defiant act of rebellion. During my sojourn there, I found them constantly debating the various theories of Marx and Trotsky with such vehemence as if their life depended on the outcome of these debates. They also believed in sharing everything including their bodies with each other, as I discovered later. They welcomed me by discontinuing their debates for a brief moment and scrutinising my appearance fleetingly. Ness directed me to the Head Registrar's desk, who was busily accomplishing the arduous task of allotting the ever-growing new arrivals to the uninhabited parts of the commune. After waiting for my turn in a long queue of loafers, claiming to be in the same plight as me, I had the fortune to see the bespectacled and bald clerical head hidden behind a plethora of paperwork. Without so much as lifting his head to throw a cursory glance at my face, he asked me to produce two references from the inhabitants of the commune. Thankfully, Ness and Hugo volunteered to guarantee that I would abide by the rules of the commune while squatting there. After signing innumerable sections of the never-ending registration forms, I was assigned an empty couch at the second floor.

'Next morning I accompanied my two colleagues back to the chicken factory. After noticing me hopelessly struggling with the batter, the head-mixer demoted me to the not-very-enviable position of dish-washer. As is the case with these establishments, a novice like me had to start from the very bottom rung, working my way up to more respectable roles. I started earlier than the other workers before sunrise and finished the last around midnight. My backstage responsibilities barely allowed me to have a glimpse of Ness in those initial weeks I spent hunching over the faded ceramic sink overladen with slippery dishes but sometimes the sound of her spontaneous and resonant laugh or the undulating lyrics of an old Tyneside or Northumbrian sea shanty she sang distractedly while cleaning her counter or tidying the tables would reach the dark corners of my little work station. "O, weel may the keel row, the keel row, the keel row! That my laddie's in. He wears a blue bonnet, blue bonnet, blue bonnet. A dimple in his chin!" I don't know why but her echoing laugh and these soothingly repetitive words gave me strength to survive in that gloomy burrow. After a very long month of washing the greasy crockery and stained cutlery, I was promoted to serve the waiters, cooks and other workers. Now I could see her again, in her red bandana-ed glory and sleeves turned upwards like in that 'We can do it' poster. She was the spirit of the wretched place. With an impressive energy, she would make everyone around the table roar with her ribald twists on Aesop and limericks using impossible rhymes like Manitoba and Saskatchewan.

'A woman of infinite variety, in short, or in shorts. She had left her native republic of bearded esmeraldan pigmies, papish *Ave Marias*, frothy stouts and soft creamy r's when she was hardly sixteen. Since then, living through a series of arduous yet instructive vicissitudes of the fickle life and having to earn her bread by various means, she had turned into a hardy veteran of the daily battle of survival. A contradictory cocktail of dreamy romanticism and cynical realism reflected in her conflicting attitudes and stances towards life. She claimed she was not a follower of this creed or that dogma and yet every now and then she would shave her fiery locks or abstain from the firewater for an entire month for dubious charitable causes. Despite having a degree in business studies, she was loath to take a conventional nine-to-five occupation in the commercial district of the town, for she believed it killed one's soul. Besides, she did not feel comfortable committing herself to anything. There was hardly a part-time pursuit she had not tried during her seven years in the big town: providing security at Satanic rock concerts, playing fetch with holiday makers' spoilt Labradors, teaching fencing to children at leisure centres, burlesque dancing in seedy cabarets of the centre. Thus sometimes accomplishing two jobs in a day or sometimes working for an unofficial ready payment, she would earn enough to trot around the globe with a backpack once a year and this annual circumnavigation was her ultimate goal in life. "It dusts off the cobwebs of prejudice, you know, seeing that all of us laugh and cry in the same way," she would often claim.

'Sometimes she would start a debate with a fellow-commune-dweller on something or the other, even being the devil's advocate sometimes, and with her impressive argumentative skills and abilities to change her accent and intonation to suit the situation, would make you believe that the ideology you had held dear all your life was nothing more than the tall claims of a mountebank or even the dog you had considered your best companion all your life was nothing more than a goat.

'If not for the stories of her colourful adventures in the faraway corners of the world, I would not have survived my monotonous and mind-numbing toil. My interest in her increased more after I found out about her passion for the Orient. She had been traveling to the shrines of Alamut and Jaisalmer every summer to take photographs of dervishes with shaven heads frenetically dancing to the beat of drums, where she would also get her yearly dose of unadulterated *charas* and *bhang*. Although she had flirted with all creeds and faiths, she had not severed all ties with the paternosters and credos of her childhood and come hell or high water, she never failed to attend the Sabbatical mass.

'With her help I managed to play small roles as extras every now and then when there was a film troupe in town. You may have seen me in some of those films. I worked in all sorts of films – curry and noodle westerns, rom-coms, chick-flicks, period dramas. You may remember the scene in *The Tangerine Fish* with the hero and his side-kick working out on the treadmills. I was lifting weights in the background. These artistic activities kept me occupied. Days turned into months and months into years and I almost forgot the reason why I had left home. I did not contact my parents all this time, which I spent learning various skills required in my profession and being enamoured of Ness's various charms. I do not remember exactly how and when we stopped sleeping around and became exclusive lovers. Contrary to the common belief, despite being *folle à la messe*, she was not *molle à la fesse*. In fact, she was just as colourful in her lovemaking as in other parts of her life. Travelling around the globe, she had picked up customs and skills of various nations and peoples. She was particularly adroit at the ancient rite of the congress of magpies. Sometimes, after our coital sessions she would play the harp, looking out of the open windows of our baroque squat at the voyeuristic celestial bodies.

'Her *joie-de-vivre* was infectious, and I believe the time I spent with her was by far the most enjoyable few years of my life. She left a great spiritual influence on me. I remember being exceedingly worried about my prematurely fast receding hairline. Initially, she tried to console me saying that it was a mere parting problem but seeing that I wouldn't buy that she prepared me dozens of ointments. Unfortunately, none of them worked in the end.' Saying this the foreigner took off his hat revealing and exhibiting his lustrous head to the company, which caused everyone present to emit sympathetic cooing sounds.

'One day, while serving a customer, my ears picked the news report of a popular rising against the atrocious regime of the tyrant king Azdak in my beloved homeland. All of a sudden I remembered why I had escaped home. Life, heretofore aimless, seemed to have retrieved its goal suddenly. The news-reporter was explaining the rebellion was fast spreading throughout the country under the banner of a blacksmith. The first thought that came to my mind was how much more capable I was to lead the movement and help my people, being the child of an ancient prophecy, endowed with the skills that I had gained while working independently, hailing from a noble family of blue-bloods and basically having been brought up in the West. I remembered my resolve and decided that I was to travel then and there to my homeland and lead the revolution. My country needed me.

'However, I realised soon that the foremost obstacle hindering me from an immediate departure to accomplish my destiny was the tricky affair of explaining it all to Ness, who had lately been making arduous arrangements for our first holiday. A joint holiday, she had predicted many times, would be a defining moment in our relationship. Despite being vaguely convinced that she would be sympathetic to my cause, I hated to see disappointment on her face at the news that we would not be embarking on something she had been so enthusiastically preparing. Days passed by without my being able to muster up the courage and utter the fateful words to her. My upbringing had not prepared me for this kind of awkward confrontation after all. My anxiety started manifesting itself before everyone and I had nightmares every night. I feel ashamed confessing this even to myself but I even dreamt of her death so that I wouldn't have to tell her that I wanted to part with her. It was a very vivid dream. It was her funeral on a rainy day. Attended by just a handful of people. I still remember their faces. A tall, serious-looking woman in a Gothic cloak with an air of nobility about her. A bald man with a blank look on his face and large brown bags around his wide, anxious eyes. Hang on, I know him. That's me. Yes, me with my once portly body carefully fed upon battered chicken gone emaciated. And a young gravedigger of an Olympian build, moving his elbows nimbly. He looks up. His green eyes are shining like a cat's. There's one more person there. A man hiding under his hood. There's something about him that makes me uneasy. He seems to be quietly observing everyone though I am unable to see his face. A very vivid dream, you see.

'That dream was a sign. I had to run away. In the end, I

decided to escape without venturing to face the possible awkwardness. I remember with much sorrow how I abandoned her on that summer night. The windows were left open to let some breeze in and there she was, lying peacefully like a russet Danaë on the carpeted floor, immersed in the silver glow of moonlight invading the room – lying in a majestic serenity like the opening notes of Tanburi Jemil's *Nikriz Sirto*. Her marble splendour was oozing sensuality from every pore of her body even in that unconscious state, like a river of sensuous delight, completely unaware of and indifferent to the effects it was having on its admiring beholder. I felt a pang in my chest whenever I remembered that last look I had cast on her.' The foreigner heaved a deep sigh. His eyes had a glimmer of tears.

'By then I had saved enough money to permit me to travel but due to the unpredictable state of affairs in Rey, no planes would fly and no ships would sail in that direction. Therefore, I decided to set off on my two feet, deciding to hitchhike when possible, towards my ancestral land, not ignoring the fact that a pedal journey would also enable me to visit many strange lands and encounter many exotic people on the way and I would be able to undergo some life-enriching experiences.

'I will not tire you with the details of all the events and calamities that befell upon my head on the road but the account of some more interesting ones might divert you. Once, for instance, I passed through a region where womenfolk were unable to sit astride a steed or a motorcycle owing to some deformity in their physiological forms and thus had to keep both legs on one side on their rides. History tells us about the Huns, terrible warriors and excellent horsemen, who by virtue of their life-long horse-rides, had bendy legs and found it difficult to walk on two feet. In a similar fashion, years of side-saddling had affected the women of this land, who couldn't walk with their heads straight. Their necks were fixed at impossible angles and they had to rely on their men to lead them on and off their chargers.

'One day I arrived at a strange city where everyone seemed distressed and morose. People were walking about quietly and gloomily as if mourning someone's death and if not for the constant noise of hideously decorated rickshaws and trucks, I would have easily taken it as the city of the dead. I ventured to ask a few passers-by about the cause of their gloom which was hanging over their heads like a dreary cloud. Most of them paid no attention to me. Some stared at my face with blank, hollow eyes. At last a kindly man whispered in my ears that the lonely and solitary hair on the bald and shining head of that realm's King, which he had kept in a jar of preservatives and which he would only don before meeting foreign dignitaries, had been stolen. A state of emergency had been enforced and the law-enforcing arms of the realm were tirelessly seeking the culprit. The King had gone into a reclusive hibernation and his eight-year-old son was representing the Crown in the meantime and according to some, proved a better ruler than his father.

'I was also told that the rash thief had left a huge blob of phlegm behind him in haste or perhaps as a sign of defiance to the police, who had taken the specimen to determine its source through scientific methods. The sympathetic whisperer elaborated that in the olden days theft was punishable by the severance of various limbs but due to the protest and uproar from many international societies of limbless people, this kind of cautioning and punitive measures had been abolished and the sole punishment for the act of stealing was now death.

'The state officials were anxious to find the thief and the hair. For this purpose, all citizens were being dragged out of their homes. Early next morning a party of fierce-looking soldiers arrived at the inn where I had spent the night, forcing all travellers including me to abandon our beds and walk to the principle square of the city. It was a great piazza huge enough to fit all the people and visitors of the city. At nine in the morning, the Grand Caddie arrived in his chariot. After humbly bowing to the welcoming cheers of the crowd, he delivered a very long speech on the importance of justice, law and such other concepts, summing it up by declaring that the wrongdoer would soon meet his fate.

' "I know he is hiding between you right now," he pointed an accusatory finger towards the crowd, "but I want to warn you that there is no use hiding if you are a criminal and it is even worse to facilitate the disappearance of a culprit. It is as bad as committing the original crime. You think that you are cleverer than law but I want you to know that we will find you by the end of the day," saying which he clapped three times and a team of scientists in white robes came forth. All the foreign visitors were taken to pristine laboratories at the behest of these scientists.

'After undergoing various tests to examine the sugar level in my blood and determine my DNA, I was made to cough out a few times. The phlegmatic matter thus produced was taken into a private room to be examined and compared with the specimen discovered in the palace and thought to have been emitted by the thief. After waiting for an interminable amount of time, the robed men of science brought me my results. It seemed that my phlegm matched in shape, tone and style that of the miscreant. I was consequently taken to the Caddie's court, which was still buzzing with the local loafers and rubberneckers. In vain did I protest that since I had just arrived the night before – as could be determined easily by looking at the official stamp on my passport – I couldn't possibly have committed the crime, which had taken place two days before but the Caddie had never heard of the term alibi. He stopped me in the middle of my protests, dignifiedly stating that science never failed. I was sentenced to death and my penalty was to take place in the morning. As soon as the Caddie made the announcement before the public, many men standing in the square gave their sons a sound slap on their cheeks, lest they should take a bad course in their life, forgetting that the end of crime is grim.

'I was brought to a clerk at a desk entirely covered with red tape. After examining me closely with his beady eyes, which reminded me of a shrew, he noted something in a register. "Complexion: sallow, colour of eyes: hazel, colour of hair: light brown, shape of nose: hooked, any distinctive facial features: a hooked nose," he read aloud. After the registration ceremony two soldiers took me to a dark and meagrely furnished prison cell, which was meant to be my lodging for my last night on this earth. There was a bed placed by a wall. I sat on its edge quietly and thought about my situation and the more I reflected the more I sank in self-pity, crying over my comical situation. How does a doomed man spend his last hours on this earth? Perhaps he cries, shouts, yells his lungs out. I can't say about every doomed man in that situation but I can tell you about myself. I cried my eyes out and I was terrified. I didn't even know what was the traditional method of execution in that strange land. I thought about being burnt on an electric chair or breaking my neck by being hanged or getting my head chopped off by the exterminator's sharp blade. I shut my eyes and thought about my life so far; my bourgeois parents, my dream to become the saviour of my people and then, Ness's milky thighs with their inky patterns invaded my mind. It'd be a great shame not to see that again, I thought. The revivescence of her femora had never failed to arouse me and in spite of my fateful condition, the more I thought about her, the more excited I felt. I recalled the pleasure of getting asphyxiated by her bountiful posterior, for she was, to borrow an old Byzantine saying by Doukas, Lent in front and Easter behind. I remembered having sucked the wisdom from that teat covered with a subtle pattern of veins. I set off on a headlong pilgrimage to her sacred grotto and tried to revive the sour aroma and savour of her *causa belli* in my mind. I couldn't hold myself after that *et veni*. What does a doomed man do on his last night? He wanks off,' the foreigner suddenly stopped himself in his intimate account and added blushingly, 'Oh, pardon me for the impropriety. It's just that it was, erm, a very fateful night, you know.'

'Oh don't worry yourself with apologies. We all do it, after all. Don't we?,' the ever hospitable Zeno assured the blushing man and looked around for confirmation.

'And perhaps you did it as a defiant last act against the death imposed on you, as a last act to embrace life or to affirm your undeniable right to live,' he added after a thought.

'But probably it wasn't your last time. What happened to you then?' Leila inquired.

'No sooner had I come to wisdom than the two rapscallions in the guards' uniform entered my cell,' Freddie resumed. 'They swore at me, kicking me in my groin. Then puckering their noses in disgust and without letting me wrap myself with a garb they took me out. My shrunk apparatus was a sorry version of the triumphant tool I had held proudly a few moments before. I had a feeling that I was fast approaching my end. I was brought in front of the Caddie. One of the soldiers whispered something in his ears, which made him distort his face in disgust. Then without bothering to look at me, he announced the sentence of a day's imprisonment as the penalty for the obscene act I had committed. You see the laws of this land were very strict on matters of immorality and depravity.

'In an ironical state of affairs I had been granted another day to live before being put down finally. I was given fair amount of food on a zinc tray twice that day and was subjected to watch the daytime television. As the night approached I was once again invaded by Ness's fantasies. I grabbed my nature in my bare hands and as a reward was granted another day's imprisonment. I repeated this rite for seven nights thinking about a different part of Ness's body every night and was planning to continue doing it for a thousand and one nights to establish a kinship with Scheherazade, who is said to have related a new story every night to save her life in a possibly similar situation. By the end of this week-long period the image of Ness's body had blurred into a lot of different women in my fantasies. Sometimes I imagined her hair as grey as ashes and her body as black as night to please different parts of my brain. Sometimes I fantasised her as a snake with two tongues. On other occasions, she was a Jehovah's Witness, a hirsute gorilla, a starfish, or a rubber sailor. On the eighth morning, two soldiers came in my cell at a very early hour. They rudely shook me awake and took me to the Caddie who after a lengthy proceeding announced that I was to be punished for the crime of multiple onanism, sentencing me to be castrated.

' "That night before I could commit the onanistic rite, a tall, bald and majestic man in immaculate whites entered my cell holding a velvet-covered tool-box and followed by two soldiers with inane faces. He nodded at me politely and showed me his badge, which described him as a Eunucher. I felt like my throat had suddenly dried up. My testicles took a little upward jump in their sack. The soldiers tied my arms to the back of a chair, and stripping me from the waist down, spread my legs and tied each of them with a leg of the chair. I tried to move but could not stir. After satisfying himself with my stationary position, the castrator opened the tool-box which contained the accoutrements of his profession decorated and arranged in the most *haut ci-dit* manner, as the French say. A whiff of strong musk attacked my nose.

' "Raw musk. I like to keep my babies nice and fragrant," he smiled revealing his white fangs. He took some measurements with an inch tape around the region between my waist and knees, showing his admiration with another slight nod of his head. Then he took a long and sturdy rope out of his box and having checked its strength by pulling it on both ends, wrapped it vigorously around my sack. He left me in that position for precisely quarter of an hour placing a stopwatch near me so I could not accuse or sue him later for not conducting the operation in the prescribed manner. In the meantime, he whetted his razor on a sterilised stone, keeping time with an old tune escaping the prison radio. It was a cover of the blues song '*John the Revelator*' by a Georgian band, Larkin Poe, about the Book and Apostles and whatnot but one line hit my mind in particular – the one about Adam's shame on noticing his naked state. I looked around for a rag, a leaf but no fig came to my assistance. Feeling sharply humiliated, I tried to join my knees, shadow my nakedness with my chest, wish that I would disappear and when nothing of the sort happened, I hung my head low and started to whimper. The old gospel melody, on the other hand, seemed to uplift the castrator's spirits for he started to sway his hips seductively.

'After making sure that the flow of blood down my loins had stopped, he put the razor under my rooster. It had a cold metallic feeling and my balls took another jump in their little shrivelled bag – their last jump. He removed the stones dexterously, sparing the rooster, and without making much fuss out of it. I felt a sharp pain down there, looked down at the pool of blood between my legs and drifted off. Upon regaining my senses, I found myself lying on the bed and noticed a minuscule version of the castrator's tool-box sitting beside me. This object brought the memory of the emasculating operation to my mind. I started screaming with pain and terror. A prison-doctor rushed in to inject some sedatives in my arms and I went back to the darkness.'

The foreigner took a heavy sigh and paused in his account. The hospitable gravedigger brought him a bowl of water. Leila placed her hand on Freddie's hand. I too felt very sorry for the foreigner for having lost his masculinity in such an awful manner and admired his courage for not finding it a detail too embarrassing to hide from us. I also realised that contrary to what I'd heard, he didn't have a high-pitch voice.

'The next morning two soldiers came in my cell right after the second cock-crow. Thinking that the end was nigh, I froze with terror and refused to stir. They took me by my arms and legs and carried me out of the prison in that fashion. Then without uttering a sound, they threw me out in the street. I couldn't believe I had escaped my penalty and thinking that they might realise their mistake and throw me back in the prison, hobbled away as fast as I could from the prison walls. A couple of hours later, I was passing by a shop where a chance glance at a newspaper cleared it all for me – the King's hair had been found.

'I resumed my journey towards the Orient and on my way found out that whilst I was unjustly imprisoned, the people's revolution had been hijacked, turning into utter chaos as I had foreseen long ago. The Blacksmith had usurped all the power calling himself the Messiah of the people and had established steel foundries in all the big cities of the land. By traveling day and night and paying no consideration to my complaining body, I have finally reached this land lying on the borders of Rey. I intend to plan my strategy and raise my forces against the usurper from here. At this stage, I am not too concerned about the practicalities of my mission, being so close to my destination, and the fact that I do not know anyone in the land of my dreams does not perturb me exceedingly. I am certain that the fire of my passion will suffice to burn down the palace of atrocities erected by the tyrants of my land. Moreover, I have printed out some maps to orientate myself in the dense metro forest of Rey." He produced a large map of the underground train network and spreading it before him, started to examine it carefully.

The Boy with a Lazy Eye

IT HAD STOPPED RAINING NOW. The electric bulb hanging by a lonely wire in the centre of the ceiling, to which I had paid no attention so far, suddenly regained a dazzling brightness, announcing the return of power and giving me a jump. I thought of some appropriate formula to take leave. I repeated and rejected a few choice phrases in my mind. before pulling out my cellular telephonic device from my hood pocket to check the hour and see if Zuleika, by some change of heart, had sent me a message, but to my annoyance, the phone was flat as a board. I don't know why instead of excusing myself then and there, I asked Zeno if I could borrow his mobile-charging apparatus. This simple request made the man chuckle.

'I remember I used to have one long ago, but I'll have to look around to see what I may have done with it,' he said rising from the rug.

'Well, leave it, if it's too much trouble. But don't you use a phone, ever?'

'What use is a phone in my profession! They don't bother getting an appointment before dying,' he guffawed and then pulling a wire from its tail, added, 'I won't lie. I used to have a telephone like everyone else. Well, maybe I can tell you the story of how I lost it.' He reached for my mobile and fixing it in a socket, resumed his seat and clearing his throat and perhaps infected by all that storytelling in which he had so far only passively participated, inquired.

'Have you heard the one about Mulla Nasruddin and the chicken liver?'

Seeing that nobody seemed willing to reply, the gravedigger clicked his tongue with great relish, closed his eyes and started the following account of Mulla Nasruddin.

'One day Mulla Nasruddin is asked by his wife to buy some chicken liver as she has been wanting to spice up their menu so he goes to the butcher's and buys some of that delicacy but as his wife doesn't know how to cook it, he also gets hold of the recipe from the multi-talented butcher. On his way back, a keen kite, who has been perching on a TV antenna, observing Mulla's laid-back mannerism for some time, dives down and snatches away the liver. Now instead of pulling his hair in sorrow, our dear Mulla starts laughing, attracting with this unexpected reaction a few passers-by, who being nosy and of inquisitive minds interrogate him why he is laughing at his loss.

' "The kite did take away my liver, I know that", Mulla replies, "but the recipe is still with me and without that it'd be useless to the kite." Well, something similar happened to me when I came to this country. I was mugged by some hooligans, who robbed me of my mobile phone but in their hurry left the charger with me.' Zeno started laughing at his own joke and then perhaps realising that his audience wanted to hear more, he continued, 'I see that the narrative of my journey to this land interests you. Let me relate it to you.'

Zeno spoke in the colourful dialect of his mountainous region where a turkey is known as the 'elephantine bird', monkey is the 'blithe beast' and tomato, known as the 'plum of the Franks' in our dialect, is called the 'Byzantine aubergine' etc. But whether you call it σταφύλι or *üzüm* or *angūr*[11], you're evoking the same berry of grape in your mind with the same shape and colour and taste, as Moulana Rumi illustrates in his Masnavi. At times, Zeno's insistence on accurate pronunciation of Latin h and v or an excessive emphasis on the guttural sounds borrowed from

Arabic indicated his classical education or it could be a hint of a mild throat ache. I will, however, strive to narrate his story in our own language without adding too much regional flavour or classical spice.

' "Although I'm still merely in my mid-twenties, the heavy mist of time has covered my origins. Growing up in my little orphan school I had never thought that I would end up here digging up the old earth to give the dead their final resting place or that I would be able to spend a few *Wanderjahre*, in an Anti-Barber Society by one of the most notorious cave-dwellers of this age, Abu Himar, but there you go – that's life for you.'

The mention of that name resulted in an all-around emission of various mono-syllabic hoo's and haa's, signifying wonder and incredibility. Of course, I'd heard about the Dajjal of Terror – so-called because he had only one eye – as someone who had taken a vow to establish a rule based on his idea of virility according to which, no men were allowed to cut their facial or body hair and all women were supposed to have at least a moustache, though I may be wrong on this last point. To bring about this hairy utopia, he delivered regular podcasts attacking the barbers of the land, who he considered were the vilest enemies of the mankind. Zeno noticed the effect that name had inspired in his audience and resumed his narrative.

' "Pardon me if it sounds like bragging, and I hasten to add that I have no such intentions, but I once had one of the most sumptuous dinners of my life with Abu Himar, and to give him his due, that man had the appetite of a bull. But let me not get ahead of myself. I'll relate to you, my worthy guests, this story of wonderful vicissitudes and adventures from the beginning.

'One of my most vivid memories from my school days is squatting like a cock in front of the entire class. I was fourteen or fifteen years old. It was a fine sunny morning...' Seeing the perplexed faces of his audience, he resumed to explain. 'But of

روگن‌ا 11

course, you don't know what squatting like a cock, or a rooster for those from across the Atlantic or with puritanical views or faint hearts, means. *Khorous* or *Murgha* was almost every teacher's favourite mode of physical chastisement back in the day. To accomplish this bizarre posture, a student was forced to squat with his head low whilst keeping his rear high in the air and at the same time passing his arms through his legs in order to touch his ears. Some more sadistic teachers would cane the squatter's buttocks in this position whilst others preferred their own leather sandals over canes. It was for both physical and spiritual benefits, we were told. "The fire of hell would not harm that part of a student's body which has been touched by a teacher's cane," as our teacher of chemical formulae was wont to say. The more impudent students would laugh about the irony of leaving one's buttocks unharmed by the infernal fire whilst the rest of the body would be turning into a kebab. Corporal punishment was administered and dispensed liberally and indiscriminately in those days.

'As I was saying, it was a sunny morning in the early spring and we were all fiddling about before the arrival of the teacher. I was impressing my classmates with moving my ears without the aid of my hands – a skill I'd recently learnt from a monkey whom I'd observed closely in a market place doing various feats at the instructions of her trainer including the kinetic act that had impressed me the most. I was so absorbed in the performance that I didn't pay attention to the fact that the twenty-odd boys, who had hitherto composed my bewitched audience, had resumed their seats and had the most obedient airs about them. Someone tweaked my ear from behind.

' "Seems like your ears have gone a bit loose. Let's tighten them up a bit," Mr Buckvarse dragged me to the front of the class, not letting go of my ear, which I thought would be saying farewell to the rest of my body any moment. He made me squat as a cock in front of the entire class. Within a couple of minutes, my thighs and calves were aching and shivering. Even more unbearable were the grins on my classmates' faces. I had been in that position for a few moments when the door opened and the *Père supérieur*, M.D. (his full name was Mauj-Dean but he preferred M.D.), a stern little man with a Caesarian hairstyle, ushered in a slim, dark boy – from my inverse position he seemed to be walking upside down – who after looking around for a short while for a vacant seat, proceeded to the front and sat on the floor right in front of me – we used to sit on coarse flaxen rugs on the floor – all the while smiling at me, which caused two rosy dimples to appear in his cheeks. But unlike other boys it didn't seem like a derisive grin. Through my aching legs, I noticed his long artistic fingers and the delicate features of his face and for a moment, I had completely forgotten my pain.

'Dara, the new boy, had soon won the hearts of the students and teachers alike due to his graceful manners. Unlike most of the boys in my class, who would wake up one morning with toads in their throats and find themselves croaking like pond creatures, he hadn't still broken his vocal chords and his voice evoked the memory of the sweetest warbling of a skylark or a bulbul. It did not take very long before every boy with a romantic streak in the school was mad about his dark lustrous skin, the sway in his gait and his rather lazy eye, which honestly made it quite awkward to look at his face during serious conversations sometimes. Many of our teachers would shower disproportionate amounts of attention on him in their lectures and there were rumours M.D. himself was composing flamboyant poems for Dara.

'I too had felt being attracted to him from the very moment he had appeared upside down in my life. I had a constant powerful urge to spend all my time with him and yet, and though I didn't understand why, I continued to avoid him like a curse. Now when I look back at that time of my life, I can analyse my reasons with the aid of whatever little maturity and experience I've obtained in all these years. Perhaps I was jealous of his popularity and his reputation of a fickle tease. His omnipresence, however, made it almost impossible to shun him. He was found in the oddest places where least expected. When he creeped into my social circle, slowly winning over my friends, I stopped seeing them.' Zeno sighed and took a brief pause. As if taking this opportunity as a prompt, the sole source of electricity in the room went quiet suddenly. The coals in the head of the hookah brightened up in the dark.

'Perhaps my greatest remorse today is to have spent those few months, which could have been the best moments of my life, trying to run away from him. I could have... Ahh well! Regrets! Regrets! Something to keep me company on these powerless nights in this strange land.

'I haven't talked much about my school and the kind of education I obtained there. It was a humble establishment for orphaned and homeless children, financially supported by greasy foreign philanthropists. Nothing like your Dickensian kind of orphanages, mind you. We were given a fair amount of food, even helpings sometimes. What we didn't have was, of course, parents. Sometimes we would hear that one of the boys would go away with an adopter to live happily ever after. These foster parents were known to be kind, loving and well-off people, who didn't lack anything in life but sons and therefore, were supposed to flood the chosen children with love, care and presents, perhaps like in fairy tales.

'Being a charity institute meant that the school curriculum and syllabus were designed to please the charitable providers, who hailed from the oil-supported economies of the East or the lands of burger, soda and blue-jeans in the West and they all were inexplicably interested in the welfare of our lands of warm waters and muslin shawls. Most children were being trained to have such independent vocations as monks or fakirs. The principle ethic of the Alma Mater, however, was to prepare young scholars to confront the unforeseen happenings of the academia or afterlife. This emphasis on our post-mortal welfare was also evident from the selection of scholarly works that constituted our syllabus. We read, for example, Theophile de Hauteville aka Ashiq Buland-shahri's *What Will Happen after Death?*, Khoja's *The Scene of Death*, Memon's *Wonderful Events of Death and Grave*, Kinder's *The Fire Exit*, although the most popular one amongst students was Albani's *The Etiquette of Bed-fellowship*.

'In Physical Studies the very first thing I remember learning was mastering the ancient art of rocking. Our physical education teacher, Mr Buckvarse, would not tire of lecturing us on the manifold physical and spiritual benefits of rocking while chanting our religious or chemical formulae. The idea was to repeat a mnemonic such as Willie, Willie, Harry, Stew, while rocking your head off and through some bewildering mystery yet to be discovered by science, you had memorised the whole genealogy of the Plantagenet dynasty. I owe the memorisation of many other notable theosophical works such as *The Perfumed Garden* and Aristotle's *Masterpiece* as well as the contents of a smuggled German dictionary to this incredible instructional method – the latter was one of the books banned in our school for containing such words and concepts as *Liebe*, *Wein* and *Titten*, deemed unhealthy for our immature minds.

'But before I threw myself headlong in the profundities of these intellectual works, I had to start my theoretical learning with the catechetical primers '*Raw Bread*' and '*Cooked Bread*'. These little gems were written in the vernacular dialect to initiate the novice into the intricacies of the creed and employed the slightly outmoded way of asking such existentialist questions as "Why art thou here?" and "Where do you think you are going?" and forgive me for boasting but I was particularly good at these questions, although not so much at the answers. Another aspect of study that I excelled in were those elusive patterns of Latin declensions and Arabic conjugations.

'A few months after Dara had turned my life upside down, the examination season made its unwelcome, yearly appearance, bringing along its usual chaotic order and forcing me to cast the thought of Dara aside and focus on my studies. Several industrious scholars approached me seeking help with their conjugation tables, offering me the most attractive types of bribery: bottles of home-distilled alcohol, playing cards with pictures of buxom girls – which were quite a rage in those days – cigarettes, tape-recorders, CD players, crudely manufactured sex toys. I, however, did not want to take any risks with my career. The school discipline was very strict on this issue and I had heard that those caught helping others during an exam were transported to some training camps where life was reported to be extremely hard. Needless to say I didn't want to end up in such a dreadful place and therefore, I resolutely refused every *pot-de-vin* offered to me *sous la table*.

'The night before the test I was standing on my head in an isolated school garden, trying to memorise my *Raw Bread* when I saw Dara approaching. He seemed dwarfish amongst the towering cypresses. I wondered how often I had seen him in that upside-down position. That night he didn't seem his usual confident self. In fact, I clearly remember he had an anxious look in his eyes. He reminded me of a gazelle, who through some inadvertent misshapening finds herself on a busy city road.

' "I know you, erm, do not like me... But can I ask you for help... please," said the dark cherub diffidently.

' "Whatever gave you that idea?" I said standing up on my feet.

' "You're always running away from me as if I disgust you."

' "I apologise for the misconception but I happen to be slightly preoccupied tonight. Can we discuss it some other day? I have to prepare for tomorrow, as you may have noticed."

' "And that's the reason why I'm here. Can you help me with it tomorrow? Please." He said beseechingly. "I'll bring you anything you like."

'I thought for a moment, not without relishing the panic at

the little devil's face. "You don't need to give me anything in return. I'll help you. Now let me study."

'He looked at me in disbelief. I turned my back towards him but before I could move away, I felt a soft feathery touch at the small of my back. I felt a tinge of sweet pain shooting through my nerves. When I looked back, he had already gone leaving me on fire.

'The next morning's sun found our school in a state of general disorder and mayhem. Most scholars were rocking about sitting or standing, trying to defeat some last stubborn formulas. Some were scribbling hasty notes with feverish hands on their calves or thighs. A few were strolling aimlessly, their eyes blank with terror. However, despite all the chaos caused by the examination, I was amazed to find myself oddly calm and confident. The superintendent, our old friend M. Buckvarse, that day was notoriously vigilant, which failed to hinder the hardcore cheaters from cheating in the exam. He caught many alumni trying to use the notes, known as *booty* or weed in the local dialect, which they had hidden in their socks, shoes, pants or breeches. He had left me on my own, however, because of my reputation at being good at all that *volō, vīs, vult* and فعل فعلا فعلوا, and I decided to avail this lenience with gratitude. After finishing my test hastily, I signalled to Dara, who dexterously threw a paper projectile at me, which almost hit the constantly ambulant superintendent. I managed a furtive dive to collect the crumpled paper and opening it, noticed his inked fingerprints all over it. I tore a little piece off and having touched it quickly with my lips, thrust it in my pocket. I finished his conjugations for him and threw the paper back at him. He caught it before Mr Buckvarse could turn his back and looked at me with gratitude in his moist eyes. When the results were announced a few weeks later, the little imp, to my annoyance, had been awarded higher marks than I had. That incident was the beginning of our friendship, or in other words, from that day onwards, I stopped avoiding him.

'A few days after the ceremony of the end of the academic year, I came down with a nasty cold, which annoyingly forced me to stay immobile in my bed. All the other boys of my class were in the playground. I could hear their shouts and wished I was out frolicking with them. I picked up a book to keep my mind away from their inviting yells. It was the smuggled copy of the banned German dictionary, which I enjoyed reading with a guilty relish. I also loved learning new words and ideas but that day every noun, adjective and verb was making me think of Dara – even superficially innocent or irrelevant words such as *Blume, Hüfte* or *Sechskant* – as if everything in the whole wide world had gathered in one point, one name, Dara, Dara, Dara. *Dara dahad dard, Dara darad darman, Dara darust, davast*[12]. That day for the first time, I fathomed the true depth of my obsession. I looked for the little piece of paper, which had been touched by his fingers, but couldn't find it to my annoyance. I felt frustrated, restive, powerless and was sobbing pathetically in my helpless state when I realised I wasn't alone. Dara was standing there smiling and holding the door ajar. I tried to say something but my thoughts got stuck in his dimples, making me wish I could remain in those little wells forever. I remembered the classical poets who liked to compare their beloved's dimples to the Well of Babylon where the two angels with rhyming names of Harut and Marut had been hanged like two bats by the Divine Wrath as a punishment for practising forbidden acts of sorcery – ahhh those little *Brunnen des Engeln*!

'He approached me quietly and sat next to me. Taking hold of my hand, he lifted the enormous book that I had dropped on the floor in confusion without realising it. I tried to say something but my dry throat made an anxious noise like the little yelp uttered by an ambushed deer. He opened a random page in the dictionary, put his finger on a word and asked me what it was.

---

12 'Dara gives pain, Dara possesses remedy, Dara is the cure, and the medicine' (دارا دهد درد، دارا دارد دارا دارومت، دوامت .(درمان، دارا دارومت، دوامت).

"*Frühling*," I said. He liked how it sounded and started humming it in his tinny voice. "How do you say hand in this language?" he asked squeezing my hand with his. "Hand," I said regaining my confidence.

‘ "Ahh, like in the *Farangi* language. And what about eyes?" he stared in my eyes.

‘ "*Augen*."

‘ "And lips?"

‘ "*Lippen*."

We both learnt many new words about anatomy. The memory of that evening still fills my mind with his sweet voice humming those forbidden foreign sounds.

Amongst the Blind

NEXT MORNING, I WOKE UP EARLY to go and see Dara. I'd been dreaming about him all night long. But I had hardly come out of my room when I saw M.D. on a veranda shouting and waving his thin arms in the air like a mad man. With some difficulty I managed to understand what he was yelling about. He was ordering all the students above five feet to be gathered in the field outside our school. Everyone seemed agitated and some equally excited masters had started knocking at the students' dormitory doors to drag them to the field. I was shoved and kicked from all sides by a deluge of arms and feet and somehow found myself outside in the open. It had just stopped raining and all the trees and their foliage looked fresh with the layers of dust having been washed away. A shapeless throng of tall boys was gathered around some seriously hirsute men.

‘ "Maybe these hairy men are the adopters we've been hearing about all this time," I thought. "I think they prefer tall sons".

'A one-eyed man, clearly the chief of the beards, was astride a white horse, inspecting the chosen students with his one good eye and pointing to all the able-bodied ones to get in an Indian file. He rode in front of each of us, quietly reciting something and without saying a word to any of us, piercing our hearts with his solitary eye. Only when he approached me I realised that he was humming the latest tunes on the pop charts. I later found out that he was a fanatic fan of the Deaf Metal band, *The Batilan Battalion*. You might remember that band of bearded hippies.

What made them extraordinary was their inability to hear. They were born deaf but, with an astounding and incomprehensible ability, had learnt to sing, or rather, howl. Their music, classified as the death grunts, had become a sensation among the confused youth of the country.

'The one-eyed equestrian, Caliban the Cannibal aka Ranjit of the Oxus, went by the popular name of Abu Himar amongst his admirers. He was a leviathan of a man and a behemoth of a beast: many feet and even many more inches tall – some maintained 7, some claimed 5 – no one could be certain of his height, which was not the only enigma about his person. There were similar controversies about his ethnicity, colour and gender. Someone had carved the sign of aleph on the bridge of his nose in a nightclub brawl. This alphabetical symbol increased the frightening effect he had on the beholder. He had six toes and predicted that his death was going to take place in a polo ground just like his more famous six-digited predecessor Aybek. He had a bushy beard sprouting from his chin and the Adam's apple in his long neck was pointy and always mobile. He was inseparable from his sandalwood rosary, on which he was always counting likes and dislikes of his social media posts. He had a hook for a hand, which he employed in various useful tasks. One of his legs was slightly shorter than the other, causing a Byronic limp in his gait. In short, he had an exceedingly charismatic and frightening appearance.

'After the one-eyed inspection Abu Himar beckoned to me and nine other children of the similar height as me, to move forward. He stroked my head in a kind manner and bringing his face near me, asked me to open my mouth. Being satisfied with my teeth, he repeated the ritual with the other lads, sending one of them back to the assembly. Somehow this practice reminded me of the goats and lambs who were selected in a similar fashion for slaughter on the days of the communal sacrifice. He gave a wad of money to M.D., who looked at us in an envious manner and took us to his office.

' "My children, you don't know how blessed you are. The goddess of fortune has knocked at your doors. He will adopt you all, take you in his long, loving arms," he smiled at us in a benevolent way. My heart started fluttering like a timid fowl. "As you must know, he is the man most feared by the forces of evil. He will raise you into men of iron and steel. Soon you will become the destroyers of the enemies of our kind. And for all that, my sons, you should be thankful to your teeth and this school. With the education you obtained here you can differentiate between good and bad teeth. Go, prepare your baggage now. You're going to Abu Himar's Society. I wish you all the best and my boys, always remember this humble teacher of yours." Having delivered these kind words, Mr D. gestured us away with his hands.

'As we were all orphans, there was no question of obtaining consent from our parents and thus much awkwardness and time was saved. We were all made to get into gypsy wagons, disguised as a group of circus folks on a country tour. Our gaudy vehicles were taking us to the northern-most mountains of the country. Engines of the four-wheel drives were heaving like worn-out mules, attempting to soar the heights kissed by the eagles. The landscape was rapidly changing from the red-peat moors to the snow-clad hills. Lofty firs and pines had succeeded stout plain oaks and mulberries. I was thinking about Dara and the evening I had spent with him. I hadn't even been able to say farewell to him. I felt that I had lost my world and that there was nothing left for me now.

'We were all transported to the mountains of Sakalia – a region of bizarre fauna and flora. After we dismounted our vehicles, a group of men clad in professional militia uniforms welcomed us. They seemed robust and hardy like mountain goats, probably by dint of the adversities of the hard, mountainous life. Despite the long journey that we had just taken, we were made to stand in military formations. Abu Himar delivered a welcome speech, which was full of fire and passion.

' "My children," he shouted with his famous drawl, giving extra syllables to each word, "welcome to Utopia, the Society of Chosen Hairy Men. You must be asking yourselves why you are here. You may also have heard some cynical greybeard that Utopias don't exist. Well, let me answer all your questions. You have been brought here to live in this Elysium of beards and taches, to return to an age of bliss, where hairy men ruled the Cave, before the world was sunk into misery, before shavers, haircutters, trims, scissorhands and razorfingers became the Devil's toadies and sell-outs. Some of you may have studied sciences and may know that hair is the source of a man's strength, energy and virility. By depriving us of the source of our Samsonite might, these Delilahs are turning us impotent and hairless. They make you bow your neck before their razors and lend your ears to their scissors and while they are at their dirty business, their tongues are working just as sharply as their tools.

' "The Devil, which has always been our wiliest and greatest enemy, has invaded us with a different weapon this time. It is the weapon of debauchery and sin, which they propagate through our own television screens. Don't think that your TV is just an innocent box, a harmless tube, which you can control with your own fingertips – no, it's the plague, in fact, it's T.B., if you pardon the pun". He laughed at his own creativity for a second before resuming a serious tone. "The venomous effects of television have corrupted our people. It dopes you up. It makes you lethargic. It induces in you the desire to commit sins. Television plays adverts of shaving creams, razors, trimmers, pubepinchers, tweezers, woolshearers, lawnmowers. Men these days have fallen in sinful ways. They sell their hair like a greengrocer sells cucumber.

' "Don't you think that these earthquakes, these storms, floods, heatwaves are warnings from the above? I have myself studied geological sciences and know that these natural disasters are in fact results of our unnatural ways and we ourselves have incurred the wrath of the heaven upon us.

' "But this divine anger won't stop at natural catastrophes. The more our sins grow, the closer we'll be getting to the final day. My children, do you remember the signs of the imminence of the Doomsday? Soon this earth will be run over under the steel hooves of the bloodthirsty hordes of Gog and Magog.

'His tone became more sinister, his words more pompous. He was thundering like a medieval preacher now, inciting his follow-ers to burn, to destroy, his eyes bulging from his sockets, his mouth spitting froth. "Hearken me for I'm warning you now. The advent of Gog and Thingmabob is another of the signs foretold in the tradition. You know who these formidable people were? These barbarian gentlefolks, related to the Scythians and the Huns and notorious for their unquenchable appetite, had been imprisoned in the notorious dungeon of Babylon by Alexander the Macedo-nian, four monolithic walls cast of molten lead built around them. Since that day, my lads, they are said to be defiantly and constantly licking these walls with their raspy feline tongues. However, every day at the end of business, when they lie down satisfied with their job, leaving the walls thin as bamboo-paper to finish them off the next day with refreshed energy, these same walls grow thick again during the night by the will of gods.

' "But my lads, soon the day will come when a child will be born amongst these mural-lickers, who will invoke the ancient formula of '*deo-volente*' and lick down the walls and free his people, leading a fresh and vindictive onslaught against humanity and that shall commence the final forty years of humankind on this earth. Beware these signs, my children, and be afraid for fear is the way to salvation.

' "Listen, my children, some of you will also be needed to for a war against this evil. There is a lot of work to be done and you are fortunate to be entrusted with this responsibility to accomplish for which you've been brought here. With the education you'll gain here, your bodies and souls will be equipped to combat the wily ways of Lucifer. You have an important duty upon your shoulders, the duty to save the world from this hairless perdition. Your lives are not aimless now. You have a mission to accomplish. You have to demolish the empire of evil." Saying this, he unrolled a large scroll of a map of the world. There were three red circles drawn around a port city that seemed to be located thousands of miles away. He poked this point with a cane.

' "This is Cardiff, the barber capital of the world; and Ddinas Road in the centre of this Celtic town has more Welsh, Turkish, Khotanese and Sorekian barbers than the entire population of Canaan and Tartary combined. We'll sack it in a way that they'll forget Alaric and Baldwin. But before we set off on this long, perilous path of destruction, we'll have to look inside our own homes. Charity begins at home and a foe in the hearth is more dangerous than an alien army. We'll have to purify our lands of the evil before we can do something about the 'Diff and its cawl-sipping, rugby-loving, choir-chanting, sheep-shearing lambskins. And I believe many lucky ones among you will have to prepare for that mission. But before that, look at this," he unrolled another chart. It was a photograph of a barber's shop front. The glass door was adorned with a generic design of a comb and scissors joined at their tips. "Your first mission will be the destruction of their dens of perversion. That way we will be able to redeem our lost manhood from their claws. But go now and have some rest. From tomorrow you will start a new life."

'That night in my new dormitory, a sort of bunker in a cave brimming with excited trainees and novices, I was feeling as if someone had stirred a storm inside my brain. Abu Himar's multi-syllabic words were buzzing in my ears, firing up my blood and when I finally went to sleep, it was with a clear sense of having found an aim, a goal in life. I believe I was feeling content with my new situation and no other thoughts, not even the memory of Dara, entered my dreams that night.

'Next morning the shrill sound of a bugle woke me up from my deep slumber. We were taken into a large room. There were cheap prints of famous Biblical scenes of people being shaved and sheared decorating the walls. Giordano's Delila holding scissors on Samson' sleepy head, Caravaggio's shaving of St John and Holofernes, his gaping head of Goliath-Caravaggio, Gentileschi's wrathful Judith massaging her rapist's throat with a blind razor, Klimt's haughty baroness Judith with half-open eyes in a murderous ecstasy, Titian's virginal Salome tempting the beholder with the shaved locks in her fruit tray, Behzad's White Div losing all hair on his horned head after a combat with Rustam Zalson amongst arrays of ornate calligraphic verses. A stern and tough-looking man pointed us to take seats and vanished after having turned on a projector. The screen was filled with the footage of a South Indian actor dodging bullets with his axe. Then the scene changed to medieval times and we were shown a half-naked man being shaved at the stake. It was a montage of similar heart-rendering scenes following one another which had been edited into the footage of the modern-day warfare for that darker and graver effect that only black-and-white films can have – scenes of evil barbers from various parts of the world and periods in history shaving their customers with sharp razors. Many of us burst into tears and kept sobbing throughout this cinematic experience. Some started retching and vomiting in the dark corners of the room. Our first training day was limited to film studies. I remember lying in my bunker bed, feeling angry and hateful that night, although I couldn't discern the cause or aim of these strong emotions.

'Training was very arduous and disciplined. We were forced to get up before dawn every day and undergo various rigorous tasks throughout the day until late at night. Besides the film classes, our studies included various physical acts. We were taught many useful skills of terrorising barbers such as the usage of a 'death *shalvar*' – an ingenious piece of clothing, which was activated through pulling the cord or cummerbund and dropping the *shalvar* down. It became quite popular among the members of the Society who would scare each other with a sudden flash. Each of us was being trained to blow up a centre of evil and depravity. Our professor of Blow-Up Studies, who had a bit of a philosophical tweak, taught us to insert a bomb in our physical cavities, which was probably one of the most difficult parts of the training. By the end of our training, each of us could fit another bomber inside him.

'I have no illusions as to why I was chosen for the final mission. I do not think that it was because of some extraordinary talents that I possessed or that my level of devotion had impressed those who made the final decision. It was rather a matter of necessity. Almost a year after I had been undergoing my training, a remark-able incident contributed to my ultimate destiny.

'Our Society was divided into two units, namely Aunties and Mates, and from the very first day they didn't get along with each other. Mates, also called Bros, were mostly men from the various pirate colonies in the world, so named because of the way they addressed each other. "Hey mate, arr, what's hangin'?" and "hey bro, keep calm and carry on" and so on and so forth in a similar fashion. They had covered long distances from different countries of the globe and beyond to participate in the holy war after listen-ing to Abu Himar's anti-barber podcast, *Rusty Scissors, Lusty Razors.* There were some women in their group too, who were called Sistas Bros.

'Mates were fond of moaning, complaining and constantly muttering their grievances. Declaring in disgust how everything was dusty and dirty there, they protested at the low quality of the fried chicken, the awful speed of the broadband, the unavailabil-ity of a decent hogshead of brew. They resented the locals for chewing on their snuff or betel and spitting colourful blobs of spit everywhere. They didn't like the way how, in the absence of western toilets, they were made to squat over a hole to relieve themselves and complained that it had caused their varicose veins and piles to bulge and burst – a fact, which incidentally brings us to the other group in the Society. Aunties were mainly comprised of the local lads recruited from orphan schools. The logic behind their name, affixed to them by Mates and which Aunties themselves were not too fond of, was based upon the way they urinated squatting down on the ground and thought making water whilst standing was the way of the degenerates. Worse, they wouldn't stop there but nagged Mates, who believed pissing standing up was the true manly way to pass water and thought their rival group as a bunch of superstitious provincial aunts.

'They, I mean Mates, were not, however, all bad. I had made a couple of good friends amongst them. One was Roxy who hailed from the port of Swansea in Cambria. He had ended up in Utopia following many heated arguments with his parents, who constantly lectured him on the abuse of narcotics. He had worked in a souvenir shop in his native city, and said that the most desirable specialties there were the objects made of sheep-dung – bags, books on sheep and their dung, postal-cards, air-refreshers, fragrances that didn't smell anything like sheep or their dung.

' "And there are also spoons carved in a special heart shape," He would close his eyes and sigh. "They are called love spoons and meant to be presented to your love interest." He was taking his time in the Society as a break from his annoying parents and loved the weather there. He'd named me a half-Bro, which meant that although not as good as a full-Bro, in his eyes, I wasn't half as bad as a full-blown Auntie.

'The atmosphere of the Society was always resonant with scholastic debates such as the right pronunciation of the word 'gif' or the correct gender of bulbul in Urdu[13]. Once I was a witness to one of the fiercest rows between Aunties and Bros

---

13 Generally feminine but masculine, according to some masters of Urdu poetry, such as Haidar Ali Atish: میں اس گلشن کا بلبل ہوں بہار آنے نہیں پاتی

کہ صیاد ان کر میرا گلستاں مول لیتے ہیں

Main us gulshan kā bulbul hūn bahār āne nahin pāti

Ke sayyād ān kar merā gulistān mol lete hain

('I am the bulbul [m.] of that garden that is bought by hunters before the spring can arrive').

regarding that man with the funny little moustache, Hitler. One of the Aunties, Tully, loved the guy and had his poster over his bed. One day, Taph, a bulky Mate asked him, "why do you have his mug over your bed? Don't you know who he was?"

' "Course, I do," Tully retorted proudly. "The man who believed in the supremacy of our race. He was a good man, that Charlie."

' "You muppet! It's not Charlie and he didn't even have a full moustache, let alone a beard and pubes."

' "Your mum is a muppet and he was a beardless believer of the supremacy of our bearded race."

' "Don't talk about my mum."

' "Sorry, but he did believe that the blue-eyed hairy men were the best sons of guns ever."

' "Yes, that he did. But you don't have blue eyes yourself."

' "Well, doesn't matter."

' "Erm."

' "Are you a little barber-lover?"

' "No, of course not. Are you mental?"

' "So, there you go. He was a great man."

'But then another Mate of gigantic proportions, whom no one had ever heard say a word before, said in a very deep voice, "It's all barbarian propaganda. He was a full bearded man"

'We were shocked to hear the giant's voice. It was more like an animal's grunt. No one dared to reply. He stood up, looked at us with his small scornful eyes and carried on, "It's all barbarian propaganda to gain our sympathies. Hitler had a beard but only wore it in his private chambers when he met his girlfriend Eva." He spat and sat down. However, this last comment caused some of the company to emit muffled sounds of discontent, which gradually snowballed into yells and shouts. One Auntie finally got up to agree with the giant and said, "Yes, just like my uncle, who wears a wig and beard in his private chambers."

'A Mate replied, "He was gay and had only one ball." This

piece of information infuriated the wig-lover's nephew, "My uncle was straight as a *jalebi*. He had many many children. Where did they come from if he was gay?"

' "Your auntie's private place," someone shouted causing an utter chaos in the entire assembly.

'Such squabbles widened the gap between the two groups. In the end, however, it wasn't Hitler or the Turkish toilets. It was the *Big Brother* show, which proved the final nail in the coffin of the Society's unity. We were not allowed to watch television and those who violated this rule had to undergo severe punishments. But I had heard many Mates complaining quietly about not being able to see this particular reality show. As weeks progressed and the fresh arrivals in the Mates' caves brought news of scandals and evictions in the BB's infamous house, Bros' complaints started becoming louder. One day they protested in front of Abu Himar's cave. Abu Himar was in no mood to pamper, what he called, Mates' petty caprices. He ordered his henchmen to shoot down the leading protesters with water hoses. Mates dispersed in panic but later that night, when I saw them huddling together and whispering in a corner of the mess hall, I knew that something was afoot. Roxy revealed to me reluctantly, and on my insistent inquiries, that the show they were so eager to watch had been a cultural phenomenon for them in their homelands. They had been following it year after year, never missing a single episode and it was against their human rights that they were being forced to miss it in the Society.

'One day, the Society woke up to find that these pirates had all vanished. The inquiry that was conducted afterwards discovered that they had been digging a tunnel in their dorms for quite some time, all the while distracting us with their moaning and kvetching. Abu Himar, sparing no time for frivolities, sent three jeeps full of trainees to locate the absconders, with orders to shoot them on sight. The teams of searchers, however, came back empty handed. Mates seemed to have completely erased their trail. Some naïve and clueless souls, with clearly no knowledge of how tunnels worked, conjectured that the Mates had dug a tunnel all the way to the various points of the globe where they were comfortably snuggled up in their homes watching their favourite TV shows.

'The number of the remaining able-bodied people in the Society after the Mates' departure was rather low now, as most Aunties were assigned with the household and recycling chores. I had, in the meantime, been fully educated and trained and was consistently praised by my instructors for my digging skills. One evening, precisely a year after I had first been brought into the Society, I was taken to the cave of the supreme commander. I realised that I had finally been deemed ready to accomplish my final mission and thus capable to serve Abu Himar. All this time, I had not seen him except on the occasional days of significance, festivity or commemoration, when he would come out of his lair to deliver his fiery speeches, always apt and to the point. On these occasions, I had always felt rather frightened of his fearsome personality and awe-inspiring stature. That day, however, he seemed a very different person. He was busy at his desk signing a large plethora of paperwork from which he lifted his head briefly, nodding to an empty chair in a rather apologetic manner.

'The walls of the cave were adorned with the trophy heads of various breeds of sheep, most impressive of the lot being the horned head of a Jacob ram. I had never seen anything so majestic in my life. This particular head had four full horns, two inverted, crooked projections sprouting from under a longer and pointier pair. But even more striking was the frozen stare in the beast's eye – a sort of fright, which said it all about what he had been feeling in his last moments. I was still admiring the satyr's horns when he raised his head from his papers, "Sorry. Almost done now. I've been trying to get my hands on some computers to make my life easier but in the absence of electricity and all that, it's just not possible." Then noticing me admiring his trophies, he added. "I see that you, like me, are an aficionado of the game!" I admitted that although I appreciated the noble art of hunting from various angles – exercise, feeling close to one's prey, experiencing the adrenaline-rush to the head being some of them – I had never myself benefitted from this valiant act.

: "That's certainly the greatest pity, my lad, for I can't express what you've been missing in your life. I hunted all types of fowls and beasts in my day – chicken, goats, donkeys. I can't describe to you the feel, the delight it gives you. Running after the prey, cornering it, seeing the fear in its eyes, giving it a bath in its own blood, sacrificing it to gods of old and new". I noticed a strange glimmer in his one bloodshot eye.

' "You see all these trophies on the walls. Each tells the story of a ferocious encounter with some of the fiercest beasts that ever soiled this earth. Sometimes I'm baffled at my own valour and courage. I started at the tender age of fourteen, when most other children were playing with marbles. I would ambush outside our neighbour's farm and catch the chicken unawares, providing an opportunity for my cronies and me to enjoy the most exquisite banquets made from the booty. Now despite its lofty claims of being a descendent of the wily dinosaur or the winged pterosaur, a chicken is a very scatter-brained bird. They never learnt their lesson, paying no heed to the fate their *compadres* had met at my hands. More and more chickens would fall in my lap. Soon I became bored of this game and moved to the hunting of rams and goats. There was more thrill in that. Rams offered more resistance and kicked up more fuss. Well, it was a great time and I have all these trophies to remind me of that. I'm glad you appreciate them," he said, looking into the glassy lifeless eyes of an ibex.

'After accomplishing his daily tasks, he rose from his seat, donned his rain jacket and took me to a five-star cave restaurant. The French cooking retinue of the bistro seemed to know him personally. I couldn't count the number of courses we had. We were served with innumerable varieties of the most delicious food that I had ever eaten or have eaten since then. I still vividly remember the delightful cuisine I had on that fateful night. For *hors d'oeuvre* we were served excellent calamari, samosa, seared scallops, bruschetta with pesto, Spartan broth, crunchy quails, lava bread and prawn *goyoza*. For the *plat principal* we had *canard confit, mughlayi pulao,* Beluga caviar, flipflop kababs, *lahmajun, bok doner,* haggis, roasted pheasant with rosemary, brochettes, blue steak and *nigirizushi.* To end the affair, we had Transylvanian *rahat,* semolina halva and black and white puddings for dessert.

'Abu Himar talked about various customs of serving and eating food that he had observed during his voyages to many different lands. After the dessert, when we were still waiting for the waiter to bring the bill, he became quiet, took a deep sigh and whispered in the most heart-rendering way, "Disney". I looked at his face thinking I had misheard him but felt too afraid to beg his pardon. He stared at me for a long time, making me quite ill at ease. "Disney," he repeated louder this time. I hadn't misheard him then.

' "The shop where they buy the dye for their piss. They all come to this cave-land dreaming about magic lamps, flying carpets and svelte Jasmines, imagining themselves Aladdins."

'He took a gulp of *ayran* cocktailed with Vodka.

' "I know you're different. I've been observing you very closely all this time. I know that you've read history. History is a burden, my son. It is a great responsibility. Mnemonics stop working after Haroun. All their names sound the same. Mutasim Billah, Wathiq Billah, This Billah, That Billah. Remembering their dates of birth, dates of enthronement, dates of death. Do you think it's easy?" I shook my head vigorously to agree with him.

' "That's why I've selected you. You know what you are here for. Don't think that you are sacrificing your life on a lowly task. I know it is a humble start but each little drop contributes to the torrents of a stormy river. As I may have told you over and again, barbers are the disciples of Satan. They sold their souls to the evil one in order to deprive men of their virility. They've got man's youknowwhatImean between their razor-sharp fingers. And don't think your sacrifice will go unpaid. A parting for a great cause such as what you are going to accomplish tomorrow will pave our way to extend our Hairy Utopia far and beyond these caves. Go now and get your final share of dreams in this transient world of evil."

'That night I could not sleep for a very long time and kept tossing and turning thinking about my colourless childhood, of which the only pleasant memory I had was of Dara and that one evening I had spent with him.'

In which Figaro Makes a Cameo Appearance

I MUST HAVE SLEPT for hardly a couple of hours," Zeno continued, "when two guards in the executioner's uniform came to my bunker and woke me up. The first thing I became aware of that morning was a strange, heavy feeling in my stomach as if I had been carrying huge stones inside me. Last night's kebabs seemed to have turned into rocks. But there was no time to relieve myself from this annoying weight. "Soon I'll be free from these bothersome necessities of life forever," I thought. The guards took me to Abu Himar's residence, where he welcomed me with open arms, patting my head and congratulating me on becoming a man that day. One of the guards fetched him a heavy leather death jacket, which he helped me put on in a fatherly fashion, before telling me how much it suited me. "Son, you look like James Dean in that." The two guards asked his permission to get a few photographs taken with me, after which they started an argument about who else to tag in the photos on social media. I was feeling rather like a celebrity despite the frequent cramps in the pit of my stomach. Then Abu Himar assumed a more serious tone.

' "Take care of this magical jacket, my son. It will give you supernatural powers, make you invisible as air, destructive as fire and light as a bird. I'm sure you know how to use it." I assured him that he could rely upon me and that I wouldn't let him down.

I still remember the glee in his only eye, which, for some reason, chilled me to my bones.

'While a four-wheel drive was transporting me to my final destination, I was wondering whether one was compelled to undergo the evil necessities of this life such as to defecate in the afterlife too and after much deliberation on this issue decided that it would probably not be the case. Moreover, the reliable accounts from beyond the heaven and hades agreed upon the point that paradise meant the freedom and ability of enjoying the pleasures of life, or rather afterlife, such as eating and drinking to one's heart's fill without the compulsions to ever expel it out of one's system. How wonderful! Where does the food go then? Maybe you don't have to eat or drink either. I still remember all these thoughts invading my mind when my stomach started playing on its crampboard again. "No, I can't waste more time on this banal physical act now," I thought, doubling up with agony. The driver stopped his jeep at about a musket's shot from *Coiffe du Mode*, the most elegant hair-dressing saloon in the town. Notes of an operatic melody emitting from the saloon struck my ears. From there I had to continue my journey on foot. But excuse me, my guests, before I tell you about that fateful journey, let me answer to a hopefully quick call of nature.' Saying this, Zeno took one of the tallow candles and disappeared behind the door adorned with the Venetian masks.

While our worthy host is undergoing a necessary process of life, let me indulge a bit in a reminiscence about my local barber from my teens – Lal the Barber, so called because he was deaf-mute and no one knew his real name. Back in those days a barber's saloon was much more than just a shop where they cut your hair or shaved your chin. It was also the meeting place for the neighbourhood's men (rarely would you see a woman there, obviously), where you could read the cheap sensational rags and hear the local gossip. But a greater attraction was the hot hammam (in fact, a haircutting saloon, though nothing like a sumptuous Turkish bath, was itself unofficially called a hammam). Hot showers or baths were a luxury back then and in Lal's hammam you could take a soothing shower for only 5 d. I still remember the sharp smell of the ever-thinning sports soap bar and the laminated notice hanging on the door of the shower warning anyone urinating in the shower of severe penalties in the afterlife. To be frank, Lal was not very versatile when it came to haircuts and the fading poster pasted on the pane of his door and containing photos of twelve Japanese men with sleek black hair, each sporting a different hairstyle, was a howling specimen of false advertisement. His price-chart had only three styles on it – *piyala* or bowl for children, *fauji* or soldier for young adventurous men and the regular for older and more serious men. But what was different at Lal's hammam, and most other neighbourhood back-alley hammams like his, was that unlike his more high-end downtown professional brethren, he not only used his razor on your face, but once he had soothed your cheek with a translucent lump of alum, leaving a sour taste in your mouth, all you had to do was to raise your arms quietly and he'd shave your armpits too with no extra charge. And as for alum, he never tired of prais-ing this little miracle for its amazing effects on tightening the loose and flabby skin, which he claimed by vulgar gesticulations to have successfully tested on his own wife. I was never good at the sign language. In fact, the treasury of my vocabulary was limited to woman – signed in that land of nose-studs by touching the side of one's nose – and man, for which the sign is, as you can imagine, a moustache. The only other sign I could make was that of cross, in both the Orthodox and the Old Believers way, but I refrained from doing so in his presence for the fear of offending him. But well, I'll tell you Lal's story at some other occasion, for here comes κύριος Zeno with a spring in his step.

'Pardon me again, my friends. So as I was saying I started walking towards that so-called centre of aberrations when, all of a sudden, I felt the most painful cramp in my stomach, which

made me sit down on a kerb holding my hips. I knew that I could-
n't stand it anymore. I had to go to the *Scheißhaus*, pardon my
German, or I'd defecate myself then and there and that wouldn't
be proper. I tried to ignore the pain but all in vain, the cramps
were just too stubborn. I looked at the saloon. The white-clad
barber was cheerfully spreading the foam on the jowls of his first
client of the day while the legendary Sevillian colleague of the
barber was loudly praising life through his gramophone. *Ah che
bel vivere! Che bel piacere!* The sharp, swift notes felt like pinching
the inside of my stomach.

Ah, bravo Figaro!

Bravo, bravissimo!

Bravo! La la la la la la la!

'Figaro giu, Figaro su! Figaro qui! Figaro li!

Dozens of Figaros were dancing *czardas* in my intestines now.
I looked in panic for a lavatory. My olfactory sense guided me to
a *latrina publica* located near a petrol station but damnation!
Approaching there I saw a barrier with a coin sign engraved on
it. I fidgeted through my pockets nervously, but I had not brought
any money with me, perhaps thinking that I wouldn't need any
earthly coppers in the afterlife. I ran out in panic in order to beg
someone for a coin.

' "My kingdom for a bowl of excrement," I could have
shouted, just like the king in the old fable. You must have heard
it before?'

To be honest, I was not in the slightest bit intrigued to hear
the story of this king with bizarre perversions, willing to sell his
kingdom for excrement, but our friend the Frank could not
subdue his curiosity.

'Did he sell his kingdom for a bowl of...?'

'No, not exactly excrement. So, there was one, there was none,
as they say in Persian[14] and Turkish[15], or there was once a king,

---

14 *Yeki bud yeki nabud* (یکی بود یکی نبود)

and God is our King, as they say in Urdu[16]. This one belonged to the legendary Kay dynasty, famous for its dandies, who used to wear their turbans awry. So, this foppish king of our story gets stranded while on a hunting expedition. He sees a beautiful stag with golden antlers drinking water from a stream and gets mesmerised by its dazzling beauty. Getting instantly possessed by the idea to capture the stag alive, he rides ahead of the other members of the chase party and soon leaves them behind. The stag notices him approaching and runs away. After riding for hours in vain, the dandy K. gets really thirsty but there is no sign of the stag or the stream. He is so thirsty now that he is suddenly possessed by the fear that he might die of thirst. His tongue is hanging out of his mouth and he can hardly breathe. Then he sees this little hut with an old man sitting in the shade of a pomegranate tree outside it. The Kay approaches the old man and after the customary salutation humbly asks for a bowl of water. The old man, apparently unimpressed by the flamboyant outfit or glitzy jewels of the King, enquires him of the price he is willing to give in return. The King responds generously that he is willing to pay the old man with whatever he wishes for a bowl of water. The old man asks for half of the King's kingdom for a bowl of water and the King in his desperate state willingly promises to part with half of his kingdom, obviously with no regards to the wishes of his subjects. So, the old sage gives him a bowl of freshly pressed pomegranate juice. In due time the King's hunting team arrives there and the King leaves, profusely thanking the oldie of the hut.

'On another similar occasion, our King, who like most legendary monarchs of the old, is very fond of hunting, is away on another chase when he realises that for some reason, he is unable to make water. Thinking it as a passing whim of his urinary machinery, he decides to drink gallons of liquid but

---

15 *Bir varmış bir yokmuş*
16 *Ek thā bādshāh, hamārā tumhārā Khudā bādshāh* (ایک تھا بادشاہ، ہمارا تمہارا خدا بادشاہ)

whatever he does, it does not seem to work. Feeling that he is going to burst with all that water he has consumed, but being unable to pass his urine, he is writhing in pain when hey presto, the old sage from the hut turns up out of nowhere. Casting one glance at the King in pain he understands what is ailing him and offers to help the King but before that he asks him the same question again. What would he be willing to give in return? The King, as is his wont, responds eagerly by offering half of his kingdom. So, the old sod puts a bag full of warm sand at the King's stomach and sings him a lullaby and in no time, the King soils himself in the most content way.'

'After the King has taken a bath and is feeling happy and light, he asks the old bugger to take his throne because he has forfeited all rights to it now. But the old wise man shakes his head and leaves the palace saying, "I do not want a kingdom which is worth only a bowl of water and a bowl of piss".

'So yes, not exactly but somewhat similar to the King I was willing to sell my non-existent kingdom to anyone who could give me a coin to enter that lavatory. I looked around in panic. The only person in sight was the cheerful barber dancing and prancing about while sprinkling water to cool the front of his shop, which I was on a mission to destroy that morning. I ran towards him in despair, fully aware that those razor-clenching monsters did not have a human heart in their bosoms. The thought of threatening to defecate in front of his shop also came to my mind.

' "You look like you have a lot on your mind this morning, young man. Can I shave your bearded cheeks to lighten the burden on your chin? Dear oh dear, does that bush not itch?" he asked me jovially. "Or do you want me to relieve you of some of that mullet you are carrying as a sin on your head. It is not the eighties anymore, my friend."

'You cannot believe my amazement. I was not expecting that heathen to address me in such kind tone. We were always told back in the Society that barbers were the vilest of God's creations.'

' "I was wondering if I could have some spare change.'

' "You look like an educated person. Why do you want spare coins? I can help you find some work."

' "It's just that I am in a desperate need, erm, erm, to relieve myself," I blushed with embarrassment.

' "Ah, yes of course, now it explains why you looked like you were carrying the burden of the entire world around," he burst into a loud laughter. "There you go, my young friend."

'Having obtained the required change, I hurried back to the lavatory, opened the barrier and entered the heaven of stench. I took off the death jacket carefully and hung it on a hook. No sooner had I sat on the toilet bowl that with a loud bang, out came the kebabs and halvas and all the other delicacies from the previous night's banquet.

'While defecating for what felt like a century, I looked around to read the graffiti on the walls. After examining the customary sketches of genitalia and feeling annoyed by the wrong use of apostrophes in a personal advertisement that someone had written up in a corner, something attracted my attention. On the wall beside me there was an inscription to encourage the squatter, "Don't be shy. Mr President does it too, and so does the Pope!" and beneath were these words written in another hand. "Shit it out as if this were your last time". I read and re-read these prophetic words thinking that they were probably written for me. The thought made me sad. I realised that if not for stopping there to defecate, I would have been blown into a thousand and one pieces by now but well, now that I had taken a moment to reflect was it really my last time to shit? "No!" I said to myself resolutely, "I want to do it again and again and again. I don't want to die. Not yet."

'Along with the night's food gushed out all those theories I had learnt and debated about during my stay in the Society. I realised how pointless everything was. Those conspiracy theories about barbers and all that *Scheiße*... I felt myself light as a feather, as if

I had just been reborn. Who would think that emptying your bowels could give you so much pleasure but believe me that day it felt like the best feeling in the world?

'I know people go along with it as if it's a necessary evil, the worst act in the world, it stinks and it is dirty but you don't know how beautiful it is when you feel you can do it again and again for the next forty or fifty years and this is not going to be your last time defecating. I had made a decision there and then. This wasn't going to be the last time I would be shitting. I went out and phoned the police and informed them about the location of that deadly ammunition I had left behind in that latrine.

'I walked to the station, took the first train to the frontier and came to this country. It was a new life, a fresh start for me. Reading the local rags, I found that there was a high demand for gravediggers. The competition was tough but I believe my indifferent attitude helped me in the interview and secured this coveted position and so, since then, I've been living in this cemetery and digging graves for the dead, not for the living. Moreover, I have embraced this renouncement as a part of my philosophy, my living ethic. I believe that the peace of this world is achievable if we desire less, renounce much and take pleasure in the simple joys that life offers us, such as, defecation, and pardon my crudeness but I feel happy every time I take a dump. And constipation – now that's a bad boy, the cause of half of this world's miseries. Those who cannot relieve themselves are tormented by the fardel of their bowels and love to torment others for it. That's why I keep all these laxatives to purge my body and soul.'

Saying this the gravedigger fell silent leaving the rest of the company reflective. Now there was more than a handful to deal with there. I was shocked by his crudeness and especially by the plight of his language at the end of his story and felt embarrassed for him, resolving in my mind that I would never come back to this cemetery alive. In fact, I'd also leave in my will the wish to be buried by someone less foul-mouthed. Thinking this I decided to finally excuse myself from the company of those foreigners with strange accents. But before I could stir, there was a loud knock at the door. As I may have mentioned earlier, hookah is not a legally permissible tool of pleasure in these regions – a fact that adds to its charms – and in the case of a police raid we could all end up spending the rest of monsoon in a dungeon. Zeno got up in panic and tried to cover the hookah with his warm shawl, but then instantly thinking better of it, proceeded to open the door with a resigned look on his face.

'Apologies to bother you at this ungodly hour, my friends.' A tall, gaunt figure in tattered rags wearing a long beard, with his tongue hanging out, ran into the hut panting like an emaciated hound. He was reeking of various underground odours. We looked at him in confusion and panic while he dropped unconscious in the middle of hut.

'Who is he? What is he?' voices asked in disorder.

The long beard on the intruder's pock-marked face reminded me of something I had seen a short while ago. It took me a few seconds to recognise him.

'I'd be damned if it's not Zoltan,' I screamed with excitement.

Zoltan's Flying Circus

I HAD FAILED TO INFECT ANYONE in the room with my excitement, realising that I was amongst foreigners, who failed to appreciate the fineries of our culture, myths and legends. I helped Zeno carry the legendary outlaw to the cot. He checked Zoltan's pulse for a while, then sprinkled some water on his haggard face, which action, however, produced no effect on the unconscious man's state. He then took a handful of *ispand* seeds from his laboratory and threw them on the coals in the *chillum* which seemed to be panting now with burnt-out passion. The seeds popped up with mild explosive sounds, emitting a strong pungent odour that brought the unconscious man to his feet, swearing like a peasant, straight after opening his eyes. Realising he was amongst company, he begged our pardon and after a long series of various guttural exercises addressed us in a very feeble nasal voice, 'I'm a dead man'. I felt quite impressed by his attention-seeking tactics, which forced his audience to run towards his bed.

'What ails you, o cousin?' The gravedigger asked, handing him a bowl of water.

'The vermin is devouring me from within,' he gulped down the water, amidst his nasal hiccups. The pockmarks on his face, the sunken bridge of his nose and that voice all suggested something, which I was unable to guess at the time.

'I am empty and hollow. I have only a couple of days left before I am to pay my debt to my Creator. But before I die, I would like to share with you, my friends, my unfortunate story, hoping that it would help other wretched souls from falling into the pit of the eternal perdition, and although this story of mine that I am going to relate to you for your own benefit, brothers, is a painful and vulgar one, I promise not to hide anything from you, brothers, for I believe I must keep tasting the bitterness of disgrace and shame that my sick deeds have inflicted on me and my family.' Saying this he fell silent, his eyes fixed at the wooden beams of the ceiling. I stole a furtive look at his body, trying to ascertain if he had suddenly given up the ghost and seeing that there was no movement in his frame, approached him in order to shut his eyes, as the tradition demanded, when he made some scratchy noises in his throat. He supported his body on one elbow and spat out a thick green substance, but due to weakness of character, ended up drooling all over his beard.

'May stray-dogs piss in your nostrils,' he summed up his annoyance, addressing the phlegm and then, looking at our shocked faces, made a long formal apology for his language.

'Oh boy! In my heyday, I could spit ten feet away with as much ease as a bird can fly and defecate at the same time and now look at my wretchedness! I soil my own chin trying to spit. I am a deflated balloon, a used French letter, if you pardon my crudeness. Boy oh boy, for four days a man gets to strut about and make noise and once those four days are over, he is just another empty vessel with nothing to say. Life is a bubble, eh, as they say. But let me carry on with the story, brothers and er, sister," he added hesitantly acknowledging the woman's presence for the first time.

I noticed how careful he had been to avoid looking her in the eye, demonstrating his old-school upbringing, also evident from his manner of talking, which although perforated by a good amount of oaths and bravado – perhaps out of habit or necessity to show his tough background – was fundamentally based on the middle-class town dialect. For instance, he never once failed to use the respectable '*shomā*' when he spoke Persian or '*āp*' when he switched to Urdu and '*vous*' or '*вы*' etc. when he needed to quote from a European language. Needless to say he pronounced his ق *qaf* with the required guttural pomp. As you may know, the ability or non-ability to pronounce this sound constitutes one of the criteria by which the difference between the vulgar and the cultured can be marked.

Linguistically, people of Saqia can be classified into two groups: those who can pronounce this most marvellous and mystical oriental sound *qaf*, known as Qafists, and those who sadly cannot do so and replace it by its common and mediocre twin *kaf*, known as Kafists. The rarity of *qaf* in international phonetics renders it the sovereign of the sounds in the Orient from Tiflis to Lucknow and from Merv to Astana. I know that the inarticulate riff-raff mock us for our careful enunciation, evidently out of plebeian jealousy, alleging preposterously that we croak like raucous rooks. But why would one carry such a magnificent sound in one's throat and not utter it with the required activity, pomp and splendour? Wouldn't that be as tasteless as having a boiled egg without salt, to borrow Kipling's metaphor, or a shish kebab without mint chutney or mussels without mustard or a battered cod without tartar? Between you and me, I wouldn't trust a language that doesn't have a ق '*qaf*' or غ '*ghein*' or at least a ح '*khe*' in it. The throatier and more phlegmatic the better, as the ancient dictum goes.

Qaf is also the name of that mythological mountain, which the ancients believed encircled the world and which Attar, the twelfth century mystical poet, declared as the abode of the legendary bird Simurgh, the monarch of all feathered creatures, warblers and raptors alike, and in whose quest he made thirty[17] of the most valiant birds[18] of his fable to fly to this mountain, only to attain self-realisation in the end and in this way teach the reader a spiritual lesson. According to some, it is the name of the

17 *si* (سی)
18 *murgh* (مرغ)

magical land of lofty, impenetrable altitudes inhabited and ruled by the gorgeous and graceful fairies, whose fabled beauty and magical prowess have reigned over the imagination of our story-tellers since the ancient times. These stories describe them as supernatural elves with strange bewitching powers over any man or woman who loses their way finding themselves in their faraway lands. Those who ever come back alive report that these fairies and elves speak a pure language, written in a beautiful but indecipherable script, meanings and characters of which are lost to mortals. They are said to greet each other with the shout of *gamarjoba*, which signifies victory. Sceptics maintain that this fabled land is nothing other than the *Qafqaz* or Caucasus of Tamar, Nino Kipiani, Mary Eristavi and Medea of Colchis, whose beauty and charms helped spread these fantastical legends.

'As some of you may know, my real name is Sultan and I am the wretched man, wanted by the law and order these past few years,' господин Zoltan-Sultan was saying. 'Before my notoriety made me the by-word of every household, I lived peacefully with my Ma and sis, erm, sister in a little town. My sister and I were twins, or almost twins since she had preceded me into this world of woe and misery by an hour. It was just like her. Always protective of me, Baji, the elder one, was out first to clear the path for me, to be there for me when I arrive. We grew up together, sucking life from each breast of our mother. We played the same childish games, chased the same butterflies, learnt to read alphabets together. Although in looks we were very similar, in habits we could not be more different. She was selfless, caring and kind. I, on the other hand, was selfish and thoughtless.

'After studying together for the first five years, we had to be sent to separate schools as tradition frowned upon co-education, rightly regarding it as the nest of all evil, depravity and decadence. This meant that I had to accompany her to her school, making sure that she was safe on the way, and not subjected to catcalls by worthless rascals, before going to my own.'

He fell silent, seeming hesitant to carry on.

'My friends, you must appreciate that I find myself in a very awkward situation now. I have vowed that I would not conceal anything pertaining my story but on the other hand, as you would probably understand, due to matters of honour dear to me, I cannot reveal my sister's name in the company of strange men, so forgive me to say that it would suffice to refer to her as *Baji* or *hamshira*.

Then he thoughtfully looked at the only woman present there and said, 'But since you are a woman, I can part with this important information related to my honour and thus won't risk breaking my word. Boy, I do know how to keep my word. Would you lend me your ear that I could whisper into it the name of my only sister?'

Considering it the man's last wish, the woman brought her ear close to the man's mouth, who whispered a great deal into it. Having disclosed this important detail to a member of the company, the wretched man resumed his story.

'Many families have a black sheep; someone who is the cause of the familial disgrace and though in due course I was to be that rotten egg in my family, as a child my innocence was proverbial. Our family was one of modest means. Ma raised us single-handedly, working as a seamstress for the women of the neighbourhood. She also carved fragrant candles, which looked like animals and birds and thus paid for our school education. When we attained enough conscience to realise that unlike us most other children had a father and a mother, we'd ask Ma to tell us about our father. With tears in her eyes, she would tell us about our Baba, the most honourable man in the world, who had gone to find oil in a desert in a far-off land across the Gulf and who would return one day as soon as he had found enough oil for his motorcycle. On those occasions, I promised her that once I grew up, I'd go and help Baba find his oil.

'I think my childhood, although a bit solitary, was not too

unhappy by the standards of our town. Sometimes Baji and I played Ludo with Ma watching us smilingly while working on her old-style Singer sewing machine. I imagined my four red pieces as my bloodthirsty army, trying to defeat Baji's yellow pieces, jaundiced with fear. I've never been good dealing with defeat and would kick up a fuss whenever I saw that Baji was going to beat me, forcing her to turn a blind eye to my cheating tactics. On the rare occasions when we could afford chicken for supper, Ma and Baji would give me most of the meat, contenting themselves with boiled potatoes. All that protein assisted in the growth of my naturally muscular physique. Boy, life was hard then.

'Things changed abruptly, however, once I reached the high school. My innocence, which was merely a mask for my shyness, forsook me, perhaps attempting to find a better-deserving abode. Seeing that my robust physique and muscular body could be used for their own benefit, some of the senior children took me under their protection. I was extremely good at climbing walls and trees and would steal mulberries and oranges from the orchards of neighbouring peasants for my protectors. I also showed great promise for bullying meeker children. Being endowed with extremely nimble fingers, I was initiated into a pick-pocketing racket. There I learnt various tricks of that art. I remember the first thing I was taught was to pick up rose-petals floating on the surface of a water bowl without disturbing the water. From that I moved on to cutting a silk handkerchief in two using a shaving Gillette blade. In short, I dabbled in all sort of mischief and soon, when the seat of the new leader of our little party of thugs was vacant, I found myself chosen and elected by an overwhelming majority. Oh boy, those were the days!

'Although the new position brought its responsibilities, it also made life even more comfortable. I remember never having to pay for my luncheon. Puny children of the class would bring their tribute to me according to the daily draws. I could thus use the lunch money for better purposes like buying slingshots to kill birds and torture instruments for the benefit of my classmates. To most of us, childhood seems like a rosy idyll. Mine wasn't too different either. In fact, despite all the pleasures that I was fortunate to have later in my life, I'd say my childhood was my golden age. Oh boy, what a callous cad I was, stumping and thumping on the colourful birds' eggs I used to steal from trees, wringing the necks of little fluffy chicks. There was no end to my cruelty.

'Like all great leaders of the past, I too had a right-hand, a confidant, whom I could trust in thick and thin due to his devotion and blind loyalty. He was a ruddy meathead with aspirations to become a stand-up comedian. Unfortunately for him, he was so pathetic at telling jokes that I named him Ivan the Terrible, a name that stuck. For instance, he was bad at timing and would start laughing himself before the punchline and then his jokes were not amusing at all, mostly relying on bad puns. Remember pun is the lowest form of wit, *fiente de l'esprit*, as the French say.

'I felt immense pleasure in devising new ways to punish the disobedient children of the class. One day, when meting out justice to a classmate who had forgotten to bring mango pickle as a condiment for my lunch, I came across something unusual. After I had made him eat dirt, the son of a gun started swearing at me. This pathetic transition a victim would undergo once he realised seeking pity would be futile, trying to redeem himself in his own eyes, never failed to amuse me. I laughed at him and my little army accompanied me. Seeing that his unoriginal swearwords were unable to produce any reaction in me, he shouted, "I know your sister's name". I could not believe the level of his audacity and the fact that he had dared to attack my honour. My companions stopped short in their laughing too. My face grew crimson with fury but I controlled myself and asked him to explain himself. "I have seen your sister." Ivan stepped forward and slapped him on the face. But the insolent urchin didn't stop there. He started calling her names. "She is a little so-and-so". I had no choice but to beat the little brat senseless.

'This incident proved the starting point of a rebellion against my rule. Many victims of my sadistic games started to whisper Baji's name in my earshot. These defiant whispers became more and more frequent and unbearable with the passage of time and despite the severe penalties I chose for them, the rebels' remarks turned more detailed, graphic and lecherous. At this time, a change also occurred in my reaction. Although, I wouldn't be able to comprehend fully the nature and significance of these fantasies yet, I started to get a sort of pleasure hearing Baji's name being sullied by these strangers. This new feeling would also make me confused, ashamed and guilty as if I myself was betraying my family's honour. On the other hand, I never mentioned to my mother or Baji how she was making my life insufferable. Our Ludo games had stopped abruptly once I had found better and more grown-up ways to amuse myself at school. Now I started making excuses to avoid accompanying her to her school. Ma had to pay for a private chariot eventually to ensure her safe transport.

'Around those times something more extraordinary was happening around us, to us. The Internet first emerged in our town in the physical form of a couple of gigantic hunch-backed computers in a dingy, seedy cafeteria. Soon it was the talk of the entire town, variously dubbed as the Devil's spinning wheel[19] or a chest of miracles[20]. Although its true powers and charms had only been grasped by a very few people, mostly young lads, our local cleric turned it into a tedious tradition to condemn its manifold evils at least once in his weekly sermon. He would foam with ire regarding this latest scheme devised by the decadent West to send our youth astray. For us, however, it was the key to a new world. It took us no time to become addicted to the Internet – such was its attraction and fascination. It was truly magical and enchanting. Boy oh boy! We were ensnared in the glossy, sticky

19 *Shaitān kā charkha* شیطان کا چرخہ
20 *Mo'jizon kā sanduq* معجزوں کا صندوق

webs of the worldwide arachnid. Did we sell our innocence to
the Black Widow? Yes, but we did taste the fruit of Knowledge
in return, forgetting, however, that our legendary ancestors had
to pay a heavy price for eating this forbidden fruit.

'I think before I move further in my story, it would not be
amiss to add that what you are going to learn next cannot be due
to the effect of the Web on me for I have seen with my own eyes
valiant cyber-travellers survive its wily ways. I wish I could blame
my subsequent actions on the Web and leave my conscience at
ease before dying but I think it would not be becoming at this
point and that I will have to agree with the sage of the old, who
says that it is the same rain which brings forth colourful and
fragrant roses from a fertile land and the very same rain which
produces weeds and thorny bushes from a wild patch. For what
is the Web, but a magic globe, *Jâm-e Jam*, the goblet of Jam, which
only shows us what we want to see but the difference between this
mirror and the magical devices of old fables and legends is that
it is more democratic than them all, being accessible by anyone,
you, me – even your average street-crier sells his *shakarqandi* or
lablabi on the Internet. I know you can argue there are still authorities and powers who would like us to be watching kittens at their
antics all day long but you also have a will and where there is a
will, there is the Web. But let me not sermon you from my
deathbed for I myself am the most unfitting person to say a word
of advice to anyone.

'Although I wouldn't normally divulge such vulgar details,
especially in presence of fine Gothic ladies, but as I said earlier I
would also like to come clean on my deathbed, so let me confess,
my worthy brothers and sister, that the principle attraction of the
Internet to young men like me, back in my days, was the possibility to gape and drool at the images of men and women
copulating in various postures. I know it sounds strange to your
ears but the fascination these images held for me, and many
others, was paramount. I'd be damned but it was an age of

discovery, a sort of personal enlightenment for us. Like the circumnavigators of the past centuries, I was discovering the coital rites and customs of the various peoples across the globe. These discoveries were also making my mind swirl through a carousel of various contradictory emotions that at that age would leave me puzzled. After each session with the lascivious spider I would leave with a huge fardel of guilt, knowing that I was committing a sin. At the same time, I would feel defiant and rebellious for being able to trespass the forbidden lands of Sodom and Gomorrah.

'I made many friends in various lands, thanks to the conversational services available in Cyberia. I was learning that those people thought and felt like us too. However, since I was mostly obsessed with discovering the coital experiences and fantasies from around the world, I would look for similar-minded people to chat. Soon enough I found myself grazing in the green meadows of online fetish parties. This opened a wonderful world to me.

'One night a chance visit to an ordinary chat-saloon opened the door of a taboo and honour-fetish. "*Bigheirati hast inja?*" "*Koi beghairat hai yahan?*" someone was looking for an honourless person. Finding this something out of ordinary, I gained his confidence to discover more. The feeling of the utter shame was something new. I felt achieving the highest point of nirvanic bliss. You would think it would have disgusted me, but it was producing the opposite effect on me, to my own astonishment. I found there were many people obsessed with '*gheirat* or honour fetish', who would command me to talk to them about the women of my household. Initially, the unthinkably taboo act of parting with Baji's name, though at first achieved with much reluctance, in itself was sufficient to make me obtain the utmost amount of pleasure. But as the novelty wore off, I started sharing details about her with these unknown, faceless, nameless men interested in strangers' female relatives. They would ask me about the colour of her eyes, hair, her height. I would have to imagine the size of her bust at their behest. Then one day someone ordered me to show him her picture. This was something more serious than anything I had done until then. So far, the cyber world had provided me the impunity of anonymity. I hadn't so far felt the fear of being recognised or ostracised, remaining totally obscure behind my chat-handle but now was the decisive moment. I begged the faceless man for a night to think the matter over. I spent that night without a single blink.

'Boy, you'd think that I'd reached the end of that smutty road but the next morning, I was myself amazed at the ease with which I was sharing her photographs with total strangers and the idea that those pictures could be spread very easily on the Web was exciting me even more. I felt proud when the faceless man praised her big almond eyes, her little soft mouth and her outwardly mobile bust – as if all that praise was directed at myself. Man, it was a constant degeneration into filth.

'But I had some swell time, and at the same time, I was also really proud of leading a double life so successfully. To the outer world, I was a tough thug, the nightmare to many silly, weak, pathetic gits but in my private fantasies, I was a meek, humble puppet with no real will left in me, ready to serve the slightest whims of these faceless men. And did I pull off this double-act well!

'Being well aware that my knowledge was solely limited to the theory, I had a constant urge to realise it in the real world. I paid my first visit to the ladies of the night when I was merely fifteen. One of my cronies, who had been there before me, had told me many exciting stories of his adventures and I had drawn a very romantic image of this encounter in my mind. Man, I can recall that day as clearly as it happened yesterday. I had put on a Hawaii-themed shirt with floral patterns and emptied a whole flask of jasmine oil on my hair to give it the lustre and aroma. I was moreover chewing on cardamom to have a fragrant mouth.

Boy, what a romantic devil was I back then and look at the state I am in now! Fleas wouldn't deign to suck on my blood. Sewer rats turn away in disgust when they see me going through the litter trying to find some food. "The pest is back," I've heard them say. Oh man!' The bearded robber sighed and looked gloomy for a minute before regaining his confidence and continued.

'Oh boy! This is not the time to talk about the damned rats. I've reached my favourite bit of the story and I hope, my friends, you'll like it too. So, I was saying. Well, where was I? Oh yes, it was not dark yet when I reached the old Freudabad or the Diamond Market as it was called – I mean the neighbourhood of ill fame. The street was not too busy yet. There were very few harlots standing in their doorsteps, beckoning the odd passer-by with inviting and suggestive gestures. I cast a selective glance around. Most women were young and dressed and made-up in a sort of provincial way. But I did not care for fashion. I am not a superficial, shallow man, you see. Some of the more seasoned ones would sing their siren calls in various languages, showing off the range of their cosmopolitan clientele. "*Canım, aşk meleğim, maça beyim, hadi gel, maçanı içimde isti...*" and "*o sanam, teri qasam, ye sarkash javāni, ye andām-e nihā...,*" and so on and so on. A few reaching their expiry dates were squatting on their thresholds in a hopeless sort of manner – a scene that didn't fail to arouse a great amount of pity in me. A boy, slightly older than I and clad in a long green robe, with his head shaven in the latest fashion, approached me and in a confidential but frank manner intimated that he could introduce me to some of the best fowls, if I was looking to have some good time. I continued to walk, paying no attention to his approaches. Seeing that I was completely oblivious to his solicitations, he moved away grumbling that I was making a huge mistake and asking for trouble venturing on my own.

'I can't say why but my eyes were fixed on a plump, elfin creature, who must have been the same age as me. Noticing that I was exploring her lustily, she winked at me. I went to her and without uttering a word, she held my hand and led me to her bedchamber. A young lad was lying on the bed staring at the ceiling and listening to the remixed bawdy songs of a famous gypsy woman, who was the talk of the town then and the idol of peasants.

' "*Viré, birader*, give us some privacy please," the little wench addressed the boy, who left the room quietly. I took it as an auspicious sign. She had her hair dyed red with natural henna and was wearing a huge ring in her nose. The walls were decorated with portraits of silver-screen goddesses in fur from Hollywood and their trans-Himalayan equivalents in silken saris and muslin *rupattas*.

' "So does my lion want to be seated?" she spoke a coarse dialect suggesting her remote rustic origins.

' "Yes, I want to be seated," I replied using the same expression so as not to offend her.

' "It'll be 100 d." I had already been warned about the price and without any haggling I handed her the red note, which disappeared instantly in her firm bosom.

' "Now, another 100 for the outsider, *baahar-vala*," she extended her palm towards me. I didn't know who this outsider was and why he was supposed to have a share in this transaction. Moreover, my cronies had not intimated about the extra charges. I felt I was being duped and was not ready to part with more money.

'Seeing me being reluctant to open my fist again, she said apologetically, "Sorry, *jānum, gulāb jāmun*. Can't do without paying the outsider."

' "But who is this outsider?"

' "Someone to keep an eye at that door over there and deal with the law-enforcing authorities, and grease the cop's palm, of course," she said with a slight annoyance creeping in her tone, as if she had already expected me to know that important piece of information. I felt flustered and my self-assurance seemed to be evaporating.

' "Erm, I don't want to pay more."

' "Your funeral, my lad. The door is that way," she pointed to the said portal.

'Realising that I had no other choice but to pay more, I conceded to the extortion emptying my pocket. What happened afterwards needs not be repeated. Mechanical friction and not much besides. Suffice to say that my very first romantic adventure did not turn out to be so romantic after all. We both walked out of the room together, I feeling guilty and frustrated, she sporting a professional and decorative smile to greet the next customer, who was sitting on a bench opposite the door of love, with an impatient air about him. She knew him, it seemed, by the way she gave him a peck on the cheek. I remember the scorn on his face, however, when he saw me, disgusted by the idea that he was to delve in her furrow moistened by a fifteen-year old.

' "You'd never learn! How many times have I told you not to lie with these laddies with bendy legs and limp tools. Have you even performed, er – he thought for a while to find the right word – the ablutions, er, after him?" The incongruity of the ecclesiastical term caused both of us curl up in a laugh. "Now he wants me to do *abdest* every time I take someone in," she slapped me on my thigh. We laughed to our hearts' fill, to the annoyance of the ablutionist, rejoicing a shared joke. This even made me forget my earlier feelings of vexation and bound us both in a knot of camaraderie. We were of the same age after all. And she had a wicked sense of humour. Boy, I do miss her sometimes!

'Before long, I was a frequent and popular visitor in various houses of ill fame in the Diamond Market. Experience taught me how to deal with saucy trollops and tell tenacious pimps to fornick the hell off. I had an indomitable appetite and could even ride a thorny acacia, if it was donning a red skirt, as the saying goes. Tina, the saucy little wench, who had deprived me of my virginity, snatching my manly cherry, so to speak, became my favourite companion of amorous adventures.

'I was also doing very well in the department of crimes. During the past few years, I had expanded the sphere of my influence and activities, founding a gang of motorcyclists, and christening it with the somewhat nostalgic title of the Zoltan's Flying Circus. We snatched bags and purses, satchels and rucksacks, bottles and cylinders, name any receptacle and we would snatch it off your back, shoulder or loins, before you've had time to spell it out. Next year saw us galloping on the bumpy backs of local mares for romantic effects. Our fame started to spread around. Simple folks wanted to believe in something and I was there to be believed in and not just that, to be revered, idolised, worshipped. They started spreading rumours about me, my adventures, my history. Some people imagined I had fought bare-handed with bears, others would swear I had turned up on my stallion to help them in their hour of need. Boy, was I a hero or what! Larger than life, a myth, the cat's very own pyjamas, the bee's very own knees!

'Now although the life of infamy, notoriety, scandal had its charms, its romance, it was not completely devoid of risk. Sometimes, in the middle of the night a nightmare would force me to open my eyes in cold terror. Yes, I, the big boy of my gang, was scared of Ma finding out about my stand-offs with the penal code, my flirtations with the petty crimes, my escapades with hussies and the worst of all, my perversions in the cyber-world. You cannot stop rumours by erecting higher walls around your little world. They find their way to break in like wind and plague. I was paranoid of the suspicious looks my neighbours would give me, standing behind their half-open doorways, whispering to each other in my earshot, their bold stares fixed at me, their lips distorted in derisive sneers. I thought that everyone knew that I was a thief, a felon, a man-whore, a pimp, a pander, a *baji-kesh*. And yet, somehow, as if through a miracle, the life at home persisted to flow by serenely inside the four walls confining my family and its honour. Neither Ma nor Baji ever found out. Boy, all the planets, stars, asteroids, comets were working in my favour and then to give myself the true credit, I was good at keeping that mask of innocence on. Besides, for Ma I was still her little timid, innocent boy and since the earnings of my sweet crimes were more than enough to pay for our bread, she was even proud of me.

'When Baji decided to move to the neighbouring city of R. to continue her studies in the college, I kicked up a fuss, protesting a great deal. With my knowledge of the street and its rotten ways, I knew it was best to keep my family's honour under the protection of my roof. Nothing good would come of Baji stepping over our doorstep and I was right, as you will see. I tried to dissuade our mother by telling her how evil the world was, how it preyed on the innocent, how it corrupted the upright. A filthy old lecher, a dirty billy goat, it is, this world of ours. As soon as our shy, modest, impressionable sisters leave the security of their homes, they are hissed upon by cat-callers, chased and harassed by stalkers, lured into sin by the pervert society, until one day they are pushed into decadence, perversion – keep your daughters and sisters within the confines of your homes if you don't want them turned into little trollops, that's what I tell everyone. But I couldn't say it so openly to our Ma.

' "You don't know, *Valida* dear, how the world has changed since you set your foot out of home. There's no innocence left anywhere. Men are constantly on a look out to corrupt women," I argued with our mother. She, however, wouldn't listen to me, brushing off my reasons as unfounded paranoias of an overprotective brother, insisting that bad or not, you must go on living in this world. Well, you just can't argue with these old-timers. They think just because they've been around longer than you, they know more than you. In short, she consented to Baji's move to the college.

'By this time, I had become so notorious that I had to hire secretaries to answer the importune calls from journalists seeking to interview me. An author or two contacted me to write my biography. A film director wanted to shoot a biopic based on my adventures. At last, the law noticed my activities too, and started hounding me, cocking its ears and wagging its tail, thinking it could use me to promote its own nefarious ends. In short, this was probably the golden age of my legend and to borrow Byron's words, I woke up one morning and found myself wanted by the police. My posters were everywhere: on school walls, shopping malls, space centres, public pissoirs, slaughterhouses. I was more than happy with myself and with what I had managed to achieve in such a short period of time. To blame me for my subsequent arrogance, saying that my fame got to my head would be unfair. After all, I was at the apex of my career. I bought a new mansion for my ever-grateful mother with a pond full of trout.

'My visits to the Diamond Market were more frequent now. My popularity had given Tina the status of the uncrowned queen of bazaar. She had left her provincial fashion far behind and only wore the high-end designer's stuff. She bossed around all and sundry without any discrimination. I remember the aura of the celebrities we had around us, when we walked together through the streets of ill fame causing the inhabitants to come out running to their doors and balconies to gape at us in awe. I had bought Tina a transplant for her right breast – my favourite of the duo. I used to call it Mephsito – as a present on her 23rd birthday. She was even thinking of posting an intimate video with some willing client to increase her scandalous fame. I would not stoop myself to that obviously.

'It had been a year since Baji had been living in the city. For her safety I had provided her with a fearsome bodyguard, who followed her everywhere like a shadow although she always considered having him as her constant stalker slightly cumbersome. One day Ivan, the general of my childhood army, approached me with an air of hesitance and secrecy about him.

' "*Ustad*, I hope everything is great, you know, at home. I mean with the, erm, family."

‘ "What makes you ask about my home?"

‘ "Oh no... Er, just wondering if you are doing well, sir, boss," he stammered.

‘ "Yes, pretty well. What do you want to say?"

‘ "You know how much respect, er, boss man, I have for you and your household."

‘ "What are you getting at?"

‘ "I, me, just heard some rumours, *usta*."

‘ "What kind of rumours?"

‘ "About Ba..."

‘Before he could say any further, I gave him a solid slap. He fell silent but I was intrigued now. With the help of another slap on his face, I asked him to carry on.

‘ "Boss, our most respectable Baji has been seen with a boy lately."

‘I slapped him again and asked him what he could mean by a boy and after he had defined the word, I realised that something was happening to me. I was feeling a strange urge to find out everything about this boy, his appearance, size, dimensions whether he was a brawny hunk or a lanky type and many similar questions which came to my tongue uncontrollably. Two incongruous reactions were taking effect in me at the same time. On one hand, I felt extremely angry at this impudent Romeo, who had been so audacious to attack my honour. This anger was also somewhat mixed with jealousy. Of course, I never once thought of possessing my sister myself, God forbid, but on the other hand, imagining her sitting beside this insolent lad made me unbearably jealous. This lover boy was apparently a fellow student of Baji's.

‘ "And where do they meet?"

‘ "In a cactus field, boss."

‘ "What in the name of the seventh heaven! In a bleeding cactus...," I felt my bottom getting pricked by thorns.

‘ "There's a shed in the field, *mein* boss *mann*. They're introducing a special kind of cacti to our land to lure some bugs, *dadash*. I've heard they intend to mix the blood of these bugs into food. Milk and bread we buy from these wily shopkeepers."

I had heard about cochineal from Marina Bratian, one of my paramours, the one famous for her posterior. She told me that the extracted bloody matter of the eggs of these insects was supposed to be used as a dye in many shades of the lipstick, which gave her lips a sexy red gloss. She had such full lips!' Sigh, cough, spit, phlegm, blood.

'So, Ivan was telling me about the lovers' tryst. The cactus fields, being outside the university campus, were unfrequented by most students, who preferred to spend their nights in squalid discotheques.

' "And why the hell do I pay this bloody bodyguard, if he can't do his job properly?"

' "I don't know, *dada*, but I fear he is on their side."

' "Arrange a sound thrashing for him as soon as possible and when is this bastard meeting her again?"

' "Tonight, boss man."

' "I'd like to be there tonight."

'I was going through an overwhelming number of strange and paradoxical emotions: anger, jealousy, eagerness, excitement, joy. To ease off my excitement, I utilised the few hours before the nightfall to visit a manicure-pedicure centre frequented by famous people. Before setting off I perfumed my hair and put a few cardamoms in my mouth. Ivan drove me to the place of the tryst and parked the car at some distance from the cactus fields. I ordered him to wait for me there and walked through the field of thorny cacti towards the wretched shed.

'I could hear their conversation – though not very loud, yet perfectly audible in the stillborn silence of the night, which was occasionally perforated by the ominous hooting of an invisible, lonely owl – from a distance. The shed door seemed locked from inside and the only opening was a skylight on the roof. As I may have mentioned before, I had always been great at climbing walls; with little effort, I managed to slither up a pipe and angling from the roof, I peeped into the shed. In the flickering light of the lamp, the shadows of the two lovers sitting on the haystack had gained gigantic proportions on the wall behind them. For some subconscious reason, perhaps influenced by the memories of Bollywood musicals I had seen as a child, I genuinely expected them to break into a romantic song any moment. Instead, I heard them talking about books.

' "Wonder what was Manto thinking when he wrote that story about meat?"

' "I think he was explaining the physical effects of a psychological phenomenon or the psychological effects of a physical act or something in those lines. Crazy times, they were. Neighbours butchering, slaying, raping neighbours and for what? Is your meat ....?"

' "No, I hope not. And his *Khol Do*[21] makes me shudder to this day."

'I'd always objected to Baji's academic choices. I knew that literature and especially Urdu literature was not becoming for people of good breeding. They only talk about wenching and whoring in those immoral books and hide it in their flowery words.

' "My, what a terrifying story," the bookish Romeo was saying.

'I couldn't stand it anymore and shouted, "Let me open it for you, you little son of your own sister."

'In my excitement, I lost grip on the roof and slipped down with a loud bang. I felt something in my foot crack. The door opened and the couple rushed out. The lover boy, who didn't seem to have the guts to face me, ran away, just like these spineless intellectual types. They only know how to fornicate with these fancy, ornate words. As soon as Baji had cast a glance at me, she

21 '*Open (Unzip) it!*' (کھول دو)

uttered a scream. Then she tried to cover her hair and bosom with her shawl. I strove to get up but fell back with a sharp pain in my foot. I yelled with frustration and anger. Baji looked at me with big, sad eyes.

' "You don't get it, *bhayya*, do you?" she asked.

'I looked at her in amazement trying to understand what she was saying.

' "Did you follow me to kill me today? Were you to strangle me or throw acid on my face for bringing dishonour on the face of your family? Would you have fed me to dogs?" I groaned with pain.

' "Have you never slept with anyone?" she continued. I looked at her face. Did she know everything about me? My most hidden secrets?

'At that moment, I felt like someone had knocked the wind out of my sails. My whole life, with its meaningless vanities, jealousies, my idea of honour, the idea that my upbringing, surroundings had inculcated in me, everything shattered before my eyes. I felt wretched. I shut my eyes with shame and started sobbing. Baji held my head in her arms. I cried for what felt like hours before falling to a deep sleep despite the pain in my foot.

The wretched robber heaved a sigh and went quiet. I cast a furtive glance at Zoltan's sobbing face and wondered whether I should let him finish his story.

Crawlin' King Snake

WHEN I WOKE UP, I was lying there amid fields on my own and beside me was Baji's *rupatta*, her shawl,' Zoltan continued in his nasal croaking voice, which reminded me of a rook. 'I tried to remember why and how I had ended up in that desolate place. A solitary owl was hooting on a nearby acacia and adding to the sombreness of the air. I felt a dull pain in my foot, which was accompanied with a strange buzz in my head, a feeling of remorse or guilt. Had I done something irreversibly bad? Only I couldn't recall. I felt hollow in my abdomen and realised that my appetite and desire had left me forever.

'I limped my way to Ivan's jeep, who ran to help me. For some reason that I couldn't explain to myself, I ordered him to drive me to the streets of infamy in Diamond Market. My loyal henchman seemed slightly puzzled at this order but instead of asking any questions, he turned the jeep in the direction I desired it to move.

'The Market was as crowded as usual, with various melodies, honeyed voices and ripples of laughter hailing its visitors to the narrow alleys of the old Freudabad neighbourhood. Ladies of all genders, ranks and predilections were perched on their balconies, clad in gorgeous furs, rubber, latex and leather in the fashion of the high baroque and conversing coquettishly with their beaux and belles in the street. "Jasmine! *Gelsomino del Vecchio Mondo! Yasaman! Yas-e man!* My despair!" a flower-vendor was selling the freshest of the day. There was the usual tobacconist sitting cross-legged like a faithful landmark besides Tina's house. I gave the three usual knocks to the sturdy oak door. Madame Lala's masculine voice reached my ears, "Not yet, she's with another gentleman". You cannot imagine my frustration. I did not happen to be in a very patient mood, but it was worse to imagine that the senile Madame had not recognised my knock. To be fair though, I hadn't announced my arrival beforehand, I thought consoling myself. But a subconscious half-formulated thought kept whispering at the back of my mind that somehow the entire world knew by now that I had lost my appetite, verve, virility. I strolled down to the ancient tobacconist snugged amongst heaps of cheap fragrances and packets of incense. I bought a little packet of chewable cardamom off the old-timer.

'At last, Tina's little gap-toothed brother came running to me. "Baji wants to see you. She didn't know you were here," he sprayed lispingly through the gaps of his teeth. I pushed him aside and almost ran towards her lofty mansion. "Do you have your gun with you? Can you make it pop?" I heard him shout behind my back.

'I walked straight to her room, where she was sprawled triumphantly on her couch, wrapped in a colourful shawl and sipping on a post-coital soda. In the past the idea of her just having been with another man had always worked wonders with me. I forgot about my aching foot and jumped at her, throwing the shawl on the floor without any formalities. She didn't disappoint me as usual. "Whoa, whoa, you seem to be in quite a mood, *aslanım*, my lion," she said with the mischievous twinkle in her eye that I was so mad about and the little tart knew it. An impish lock of hair was falling on her left cheek and she kept pushing it with the back of her hand. Her young, plump thighs had bite marks on them. Oh how I miss my little Tina! We lay down in a tight embrace, I in a mad frenzy, she responding with all her body to my fast dwindling rhythm.

' "No, it's not going to work. Let's try something else," I

suggested realising with dread that I was still limp and lifeless. As usual, she gladly agreed to all my wishes but alas, whatever we did, produced the same result. At last, I gave it up, "No, no, no, it's no use. I know, I know what's happened to me". Tina was staring at my face. I had never failed her before.

' "You look tired. Maybe, it's just exhaustion. Let me get you a glass of warm milk with almonds and poppy seeds and in no time, you'll be ready like a stallion," she winked at me, holding me in her hands. I jumped away from her and screamed almost hysterically, "Didn't I say, it's all pointless? I've been cursed. I am impotent."

'I left her bewildered and flustered and ran out of that wretched place. I kept running for a long time, not knowing or caring about where I was heading. It had started to rain heavily. Rain and wind were lashing my face, but I carried on, only stopping when I could go no further. After panting for a while to recover my breath, I realised with wonder that my feet had somehow taken me back to that same spot where I had left my sister. Why and how I had ended up there I did not know. Perhaps to beg her forgiveness, or somehow seek redemption. Everything was still there as I had seen it a few hours before: the dense woods resonant with the occasional hooting of a solitary owl, the cacti on their proud, vigilant guard standing with their prickly heads and the cursed shed. But there was no trace of Baji, or even her shawl, which I was certain of having left there. I rubbed my eyes in disbelief.

'I don't know how long I kept running in circles trying to find her and every time ending up at the same bloody place. At length, I collapsed with exhaustion, losing consciousness. I was awakened instantly by someone's warm breath over my face. I opened my eyes to find Baji's concerned face bending over me. Her eyes seemed puffy and red, as if she had been crying. She took my head in her lap.

' "What have you done, *bhayya*? Why did you do it?" she

stroked my hair. I made an attempt to move but couldn't stir an inch. I felt helpless. She got up with a scornful smile on her face. For the first time in my life I realised how similar we looked despite the obvious biological differences. She, standing there, was the same person as me, lying immobile and paralysed. I tried to move my tongue to express my grief or regret but was only capable of making a few impotent bubbles. She sat on my chest, bringing her face close to mine. Her brow was knitted in a vengeful arch. She tore open my mouth wide with her thumbs and placing her mouth on it, drew in a long breath. I felt as if she was drawing my soul with it. My mind started shutting down, everything around me blurring in a haze.

' "You disgust me," she said and vomited warm green liquid in my mouth.

' "*Balā, balā!*" the noise of several people stamping and tramping around me woke me up. They had long bamboo canes in their hands, which they were employing to hit the ground in a panicked and disorderly fashion. Two men ran to me and said in frightening tones, "You've been bitten by a *balā*". That name was sufficient to evoke fright in my mind. I had only heard about this snake in fables, according to which, the venom that she spat in the mouths of her victims could cause blindness, paralysis and death within a day. Some legend-bearers even claimed that if a stone were injected with her venom, it would dissolve and shatter into one thousand and one minute pieces as if it had been made out of crystal. I had agonising, burning pains in my throat, which felt as if it had been scorched with a torch.

'The two men exchanged concerned glances and then addressed me, "The only way to save you would entail scratching your throat with a sharp, pointy device to extract all the venom out of it. Every last drop. Now, that might mean a lot of pain but there is no other choice". The pain in my throat stopped me from emitting any sound and I could merely nod to show my consent. 'They hung me upside down from my feet by a sturdy branch of an ancient tree. One of them snapped a thin twig off the tree and with a small penknife sharpened its point. I was made to open my mouth and the man inserted the pointy edge in it.

' "Are you ready?" they inquired. I was frightened for my life.

'In the meantime, the other members of the search party returned, hoisting the canes frantically.

' "She's given us the slip," they said. I wondered whether they were referring to the snake or Baji.

' "Th'top, th'top." An old man with a mysterious air of wisdom about him, probably the chief of the serpent-chasing clan, came forward in haste and persuaded the two men not to stab me in the throat. It took him a great deal of persuasion and proverbs and fine snippets of folk wisdom to finally convince them to desist from extracting the venom from my throat – especially since he had a very strong lisp, in fact, one of the strongest that I'd ever encountered – for they were hell-bent on it.

' "No, it won't do. You'll kill him with pain before the poithon doth it. We'll have to try thomething elthe." Saying this he went into a meditative trance. After a while, he opened his eyes and yelled, "Eureka. No... Camel's pith. Yeth!"

I was taken off the tree at the sibilant orders of the wise old-timer and a pungent ewer brimming with camel urine was brought close to my nose.

' "We keep all kind of odd singth at hand, in cathe thomeone getth bitten by a thnake," he explained patiently.

'I found the smell revolting and attempted to move away from the ewer. Seeing that I was unready to cooperate, the unsuccessful serpent-chasers tied me again to the tree and forced the urine down my throat. It tasted like an insipid and bland, gasless soda-drink, and as soon as it reached my stomach, I felt someone was punching me from inside. I retched and vomited for hours on end and my internal and external organs felt like they were coming out of my mouth. After monitoring the forceful passage of the frothy liquid down my oesophagus, my well-wishers abandoned me in my own vomit. By the dawn, I had a fever and broke into a cold sweat. I was feeling slightly better. I crawled back to the town and stayed at Ivan's for some nights.

'My greatest concern, as you can imagine, was the curse, my impotency, which I knew meant the end of my legend. I had to cure it instantly. I started seeking a remedy. I went to the most famous physician in our land, who gave me some ointment extracted from a fire salamander's liver. I was to use it on my private and public parts for forty days. I also ate the olfactory tongue of a Nile monitor, fried in a horned lizard's saliva with an iguana's lungs, in short, something or the other of all the crawling, creeping creatures that resemble a phallus. However, it was not to be. I was not treated by the great man's medicine. Seeing that the professional medicine was of no help, I went to the quacks. But my star was in decline, as the saying goes.'

The outlaw sighed and went quiet. It finally dawned upon me in the flickering light of the candle that it was syphilis that had broken the bridge of the impotent narrator's nose, thus giving that nasal tone to his voice.

A Matter of Honour

'FOLLOWING THE PATTERN set by my virility, my luck started to wane too,' Zoltan was declaring in his sonorous voice. 'One day Ivan brought the news that the police were hunting for me. My old cronies shunned me. I tried to see Tina many times, but she always happened to be occupied. As if impotency was not enough, the excesses of my earlier days started haunting me. I must have offended the Gallic race in some past incarnation, for they avenged by sending me their disease. My nose started to dissolve, as you may have already noticed.

'I was running out of means to support myself and although Ivan never complained, the little wench, he was living with, did not attempt to conceal the fact that I was a burden on their economy, which caused no small number of domestics between the couple. Realising how awkward my presence in his house was becoming for him, I left him quietly one night and taking advantage of the dark, went to see my mother.

'I was shocked to see her. She seemed ancient. I hadn't visited her for so long that I couldn't recognise her at first. She had turned into a handful of dry bones. She had started making candles once again but her failing eyesight was proving detrimental in that task. Although she never once mentioned Baji, I had a guilty feeling that she knew that I had something to do with her disappearance. I couldn't bear to stay there but before I could leave, she stopped me.

' "I've never told you how your father actually died," she said.

"I think now may be the best time to tell you his story."

'I was amazed at first. She had rarely talked about her husband to us in the past and all we knew about him was that he had disappeared in the Arabian Desert while hunting for oil. The fact that she thought this was the appropriate time to talk about him was perplexing. I was, nonetheless, curious to know about my father.

' "We used to live in the northern parts of this country back then, whence we had to move later to this town. Your father was a very passionate man. He believed in the old-school values of loyalty, friendship and always kept his word. "A real man always keeps his word," he used to say. He had a very close friend, a glover. His real name was something or other Khan, I can't remember, but being a fan of *The Godfather*, he preferred Caan. Your baba and Caan were always together and people used to call them one soul in two bodies. There were rumours that they were more than just friends. I knew that it wasn't true but I was still jealous of their friendship. We had just been married, you know, and from the first day, I felt as if I had been married to two men.

' "I'd always been perturbed by a strange feeling that Namus, your father, had secrets that he didn't share with me. I later found out that his chum had introduced him to the glue and that he had become addicted to its smell and all those times that he'd sworn to me he'd been visiting his estates, they'd both been in fact frequenting underground glue dens where they were served industrial solvents in earthen bowls to be inhaled for a few dāms[22]. Now, one night while they were under the influence of the wretched gum, they are said to have made a pact, which I found out about later.

' "The two friends were reminiscing about the good old days they had spent together since they had been little children. Caan reminded Namus of the times they had spent in brothels and taverns sleeping with the same trollops and drinking from the

22 A Saqian unit of money, equivalent to drachma or dirham

same goblet. Then he sighed, "Things are not the same now. We are not two souls in one body."

' "What do you mean by that?" Namus asked his friend.

' "Well, since you have married and gone to get a bride, you don't spend as much time with me."

' "Well, that's not true as I am always with you."

' "But you've become selfish."

' "I am not selfish."

' "Don't you remember we had made a promise on our eighteenth birthday that we were going to share everything?

' "Of course, I remember."

' "You know that if I married today, I would not flinch from sharing my conjugal bed with you."

'Namus, bless his soul, became quite restless and pensive at this sudden and unexpected statement by his friend.

' "Yes, but I would never ask you to do that," he said after a thoughtful pause.

' "Well, yes, but it's a matter of principle, not what you'd do or not do."

' "Yes, but we can make exceptions."

' "We've never made exceptions in the past. Why now?"

' "Do you, er, love my wife?"

' "No. Besides, that's not the question."

' "Right. Let's leave it then."

' "Why do we leave it? I thought you were a man of your word."

' "That I am indeed."

' "Well, then, why don't we prove it?"

' "Namus sank into another reflective pause. "Hmmm, I'll prove to you that I'm a real man. A man of my word."

' "And what if your wife doesn't agree to that?"

' "You can leave that to me. I'll, erm, bring her round."

' "And what if you don't remember it tomorrow when you've returned to your senses."

' "Let's remember to remember it then that I've given you my word."

' "They decided there and then to get a permanent token of their promise carved in their memory. They went to a tattoo parlour, where each got half of my name carved on their chests right above their hearts.

' "The next few days I found Namus very quiet and reflective. He was also very irritable whenever I tried to inquire what was disturbing his solitude. Then one day he bought me a very beautiful pendant. I instantly forgot about his odd conduct of the past few days, feeling thankful that the burden which had bent his neck must have been lifted. I was trying the pendant in the mirror when he said suddenly, "I want to ask you something." I looked at him inquiringly."

' "What do you think about Caan?"

' "I don't know. That he's been a good friend of yours."

' "Suddenly he burst into tears and divulged his embarrassing pledge to me. At first, I was amazed at his proposition, but he assured me it was only to take place one time and that it would save him his face and word. In the end, somehow, I felt pity on the man and consented to help him keep his manly word. The next night I shared my bed with the two friends. I thought sex and love were two different matters. While I was sharing my body with his friend I still only loved your father.

' "I thought that the matter was over now. But after that night your father started having nightmares. He would wake up every night screaming in terror. I realised he was probably feeling guilty and tried to console him, but he was not well. He stopped seeing his friend too. This carried on for a long time. I suggested seeing a therapist, but he ignored my advice.

' "One night I found out that I was pregnant. He had been out that day and I had been waiting eagerly for him to tell him the happy tidings but as he didn't return till midnight, I went to sleep. I woke up hearing something fluttering near my bed. He was standing there staring at me. I still remember the strange, unearthly look in his wide-open eyes. His face was white with terror.

' "I killed him," he whispered to me. "I couldn't bear it anymore. Stabbed him with my own hands," he showed me the bloody pair. I was frightened, not knowing what to say to him. Somehow, I gathered my senses and calmed him down.

' "He was my best friend and I killed him," he started sobbing. He cried like a child for a long time. I told him that I was pregnant. He became very quiet all of a sudden, as if the news had changed something. There was a look of determination in his eyes. In the morning he went to the police station and made an honest confession before the law. The trial went on for a few months. His self-incrimination was enough for the jury to condemn him. He was awarded capital punishment.

' "The night before he was to be hanged till death, I went to see him. He was calm and resolute. "I did it for my honour," he declared. I didn't know what to say. The next morning, they brought his body back. There were marks of the noose around his neck. His white tongue was hanging out of his mouth and his eyes were bulging, which gave his face a very grotesque expression. Women from the neighbourhood were gathered there to help me with the mourning rites but as soon as they saw his face, they slipped away in fright. "Look at his face. He seems like he has already seen the hell's fire," I heard them whispering. I was furious. After your father's funeral, I couldn't stand the evil tongues of neighbours spitting their venom into my ears and moved here to this town to start a new life.

' "Now, listen carefully. Let me tell you why I was telling you this story. I know about your deeds and it is most likely that sooner or later they will get you. But I want you to remember this. When they hang you, keep your mouth and eyes shut. I don't want to see that grotesque, unnatural face again. I don't want to hear those terrible things talked about you. I don't want to leave this place at this age. I just want to die in peace." My mother stopped talking and left the room. I was slightly upset. She had finally told me the truth about my father, after keeping it a secret from us till now, and why now? Only to tell me that she wanted me to keep my mouth and eyes shut at my last moment. I slipped away from that wretched place quietly. For many months I wandered about in streets trying to dodge the law, but I know that I can't anymore.

'Since that fateful night my sister visits me in dreams every night, sometimes in her own form, sometimes like a stone-shattering snake. She empties her fluids inside me in the same fashion as she had done the first night. Now I cannot look into the water because I see her floating reflection crying and moaning in it. I'm tired of all this and want to die now. The thoughts of death brought me to this cemetery tonight. But before I die, I wanted to share my dreadful story with someone. Thanks, my friends, for listening to my words. Now I can perhaps die in peace.' The outlaw heaved another sigh and shut his eyes.

I looked at the grave-digger's face, who looked concerned. It's not every day that you find a spiritual Goth, a foreign Messiah and an outlaw with bizarre notions about honour under your roof puking out their stories at you. I thanked my stars that I didn't live in a cemetery. It had stopped raining. The birds were chirping about outside the stuffy, story-filled cottage, hailing the arrival of the dawn.

Suddenly my mobile decided to break the silence by announcing a call from Zuleika. I bowed to everyone present and excusing myself, left the gravedigger's hut.

'Why, Zulu, what made you think of us?'

'I might come back. Are you still working on that paper of yours?'

'Yes... no, no. Erm, did you see the ending of the Tache Show last night?'

'I think I'm pregnant.'

I looked back at the dim light peeping out of the hut and thought, 'Will they lend their ears to my story?'

Acknowledgements

The inspiration for Genghis Khan's moustache came from the myriad of feudal characters portrayed as sporting fantastic moustaches on Pakistan Television in the eighties and nineties, especially that of Chaudhary Hashmat, in drama serial *Waris*, written by Urdu poet and playwright, Amjad Islam Amjad.

I owe gratitude to James Joyce for lending me his caliph's hood on that remarkably torrential monsoon night and to Jorge Luis Borges's *Book of Imaginary Beings* for adding substance to the list of spirits in Chapter 4.

The character of Freddy derives from the story of Fereydun and Zahhak in Firdowsi's *Shahnama* as well as, more recently, from a 2009 article by Iranian American writer, Ari Siletz, who quotes 'Skeptipedia Iranica', defining 'Fereydoonism as the expatriate urge to commandeer an uprising once it has already been started in his country of birth. Characteristic of this condition is the false sense in the expatriate that he/she represents the authentic native, having escaped the cumulative cultural and political mutations affecting those who stayed behind.' The article can be read online on www.iranian.com.

Parts of the story of Zoltan were inspired by Urdu afsana ('short story'), Thanda Gosht ('Cold Meat') by Saadat Hasan Manto. I am indebted to all of the above and many other writers, mentioned in the book or otherwise, whose works have been a source of inspiration to me.

The footnotes were added to explain regional or arcane information in the accounts of the four eponymous narrators. Though not universally applied, efforts were made, where deemed helpful for the reader's comprehension or enjoyment of the work, to translate and transliterate phrases, sayings and poetry from various Eastern languages used in the text, including Persian, Urdu, Saraiki and Turkic.